DELICIOUS

MELISSA SCHROEDER

Cover Art
MOONSTRUCK COVER DESIGN

Edited by
NOEL VARNER

*Pam —
May all your
endings be happy*

Contents

About Delicious

Allison Bradley has always known what she wanted.

At thirteen, I decided to be a nurse. That very same year, I fell in love with Ed Cooper. Sure, I was barely a teenager and he was one of my older brother's buddies from boot camp. I didn't care. I was in love or lust...or something. He consumed my every waking thought. Sadly, fifteen years later, I'm still infatuated and he sees me as a little sister.

Baker Ed Cooper has a problem.

When she was a teenager, Allison was a sweet nuisance. Now, I want to take a bite of her to see just how sweet. I'm beyond infatuated with her but she's my best friend's little sister. Definitely against the bro code. Every time she comes into our shop—which is just about every freaking day—I lust after her. If her brother knew, he would definitely kill me.

One drunken kiss changes everything.
The moment Allison's mouth hits mine, I know there's no going back. Just one taste of her turns me into an addict. Even though I know I'm not good enough for her, once I've had her in my bed, I know I'm not giving her up.

Warning: This story includes so much sweetness from the strawberry lemonade cupcakes to the sexy giant of a baker you might end up with cavities. There are meddling best friends, an older brother who needs to get his own life, and so much frosting used in inappropriate ways you'll probably die of embarrassment. Or I will. Maybe not. Listen, just buy the book and get ready for sweet, hot, over the top kind of romance that will leave you craving for more than cupcakes. You're welcome.

THE SANTINIS

Leonardo

Marco

Gianni

Vicente

A Santini Christmas

A Santini in Love

Falling for a Santini

One Night with a Santini

A Santini Takes the Fall

A Santini's Heart

Loving a Santini

SEMPER FI MARINES

Tease Me

Tempt Me

Touch Me

The Semper Fi Marines Collection

THE FITZPATRICKS

The Lost Night-free prequel

At Last

TASK FORCE HAWAII

Seductive Reasoning

Hostile Desires

Constant Craving

Tangled Passions

Wicked Temptations

Task Force Hawaii Vol 1

TEXAS TEMPTATIONS

Conquering India

Delilah's Downfall

THE ELDRIDGES OF TEXAS

Scorched

SPIES, LIES, and ALIBIS

The Boss

ONCE UPON AN ACCIDENT

An Accidental Countess

Lessons in Seduction

The Spy Who Loved Her

Once Upon an Accident Bundle

THE CURSED CLAN

Callum

Angus

Logan

Fletcher

Anice

BY BLOOD

Desire by Blood

Seduction by Blood

BOUNTY HUNTER'S, INC

For Love or Honor

Sinner's Delight

TELEPATHIC CRAVINGS

Voices Carry

Lost in Emotion

Hard Habit to Break

Bundle

CONNECTED BOOKS

The Hired Hand

Hands on Training

A Calculated Seduction

Going for Eight

SINGLE TITLES

Grace Under Pressure

Her Mother's Killer

The Last Detail

Operation Love

Chasing Luck

The Seduction of Widow McEwan

Snowbound Seduction

Hawaiian Holidays

Sweet Patience

COMING SOON

Delicious

Luscious

Scrumptious

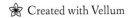

Acknowledgments

I always say that no book is built by just me. There are tons of people cheering me on and helping me along the way.

First, Joy Harris who helped come up with the idea on the way back from Readers and Rebels. I said I wanted to do something fun and different. We thought three military dudes opening a cupcake shop fit the bill.

To Moonsruck Designs who captured my heroes and the feel of the books perfectly.

A big thanks to Brandy Walker who is always ready to be my sounding board.

I can never thank Noel Varner enough for all the help she gives me when editing the book.

A shout out to both RS Gray and Pippa Grant. They don't know me, but they helped me get my humor mojo back through their wonderful books (check them out, seriously).

Hey, Addicts! Thanks for always having my back and helping me laugh along the way.

And especially to my partner in crime, Les, who has always been supportive, especially these last couple of years.

Dedication

To the real Nurse Allison. Through the horrible months of my treatment, you were always an angel in scrubs. Les and I would have never made it through chemo without you.

DELICIOUS

CAMOS&CUPCAKES BOOK ONE

MELISSA SCHROEDER

Chapter One

Allison

I don't know when I fell in love with Ed Cooper.

Scratch that.

I do know. I was thirteen and my brother brought his friend back from basic training. Ed was tall, sweet, and had red hair. RED HAIR. I've always had a thing for guys with red hair. Okay, it all sort of started with Ed, but I'd always found redheads attractive. While friends were drooling over Harry Potter—who was out as an infatuation because he shares a name with my brother—I was crushing on the Weasley twins. Not Ron because, well, he's Ron and he whines, and I don't like whiners. Also, why would I ever want a boyfriend who thought a rat was a good companion pet? And, said pet wasn't really a rat.

But I digress. Back to my infatuation.

Ed Cooper, delectable ginger.

Now that I'm within spitting distance of my thirties, I realize, it's a little stupid to be *this* infatuated with a man who treats me like his little sister. Wait, does that say something about me? *Ew, don't go there, Allison.*

My infatuation has gotten worse with each passing year. It isn't like I haven't had dates or that I'm pining away saving my virginity for him. I've had sex. Lots of it. Okay, not a lot...only with two guys...and it was pretty boring with both of them. I'm not a virgin, which was the point of my comment.

I step into the mansion that has been renovated into a small mall of sorts. It sits in the heart of the King William District in San Antonio that is dominated by gothic architecture. It's become a hip kind of place for specialty shops and restaurants. It's why my brother and his two friends, Fritz O'Bryan and Ed Cooper, decided to open Camos and Cupcakes there. Close enough to the military bases but also in an area that a lot of tourists frequent. I tend to be here several days a week. I step into the bakery and draw in a deep breath, letting the sugary sweetness fill my senses and buoy my spirits. This is the first day of my staycation. I love to travel and the fact that I cannot really do that this year is kind of a bummer. I bought my house last year, and this year I saved up to buy my brand-new Malibu with all the bells and whistles, so I honestly couldn't afford a real vacation. Plus, the only time I could get off for a while is next week. Neither of my friends can go, and I'm just not the sort of woman who would go on vacation by myself. I would get bored, because I like to share experiences. And talk. A lot.

So, I'm here to kick off my staycation with a treat.

There's a crowd but that's normal. This place is

always hopping on Saturday mornings. It doesn't take me long to find Ed. He's hard to miss in any crowd. He tops 6'4" but it isn't that. I know that I would be able to find him anywhere. And, all that red hair helps. It's longer now than when he was in the military and is given to curl. I'd love to slip my fingers through the silky strands. I curl my fingers into my hand to control the need. Another aspect of his new life is the full beard. I've never been a woman who likes a man with facial hair, but I love it on Ed. As usual, he's wearing an apron with the title of their bakery splashed across the front of it. Flour and chocolate color the white material. He's been busy, as he is five days a week. See, Ed Cooper just isn't only the man I've been in love with for fifteen years. He's a baker. A cupcake baker. And not just any cupcake baker. He's considered one of the top bakers in San Antonio. Five days a week, he creates sugary, decadent treats.

I call him my own personal Ginger Jesus.

Now, you might be thinking that he's some kind of wimpy kind of guy. Not that I think bakers are wimpy, but Ed is probably the opposite of what most people would think of a baker. He's sexy as sin, tatted up with skulls, still sports a six-pack, and rides a Harley.

I watch him scan the bakery, looking over the customers. There's more than a shop keeper's interest to his gaze, which makes sense. Ed, Fritz, and my brother are all former Army. They inspect areas the same way whether they are in the shop or out on the River Walk. They cannot help it. Some things just become second nature, even after trading their uniforms for aprons.

The moment his gaze settles on me, my body temperature escalates into overheating territory. A slow, sexy smile curves his lips. Oh, goodness. Just like the first time he looked at me, I feel my heart dance a little jig and my face heats up, not to mention my pussy tightening. I walk around with wet panties whenever I'm near Ed. Or thinking about him. So, like, almost all the time.

I remind myself that he isn't for me, never will be. He's...unattainable. He'll always see me as that flat-chested, frizzy-haired teenager who couldn't say hi to him without blushing.

Same story, different decade—although with boobs and better hair.

Anytime I complain about the lack of sex in my life, my best friend EJ claims I will never find another man. Not while I'm infatuated with Ed. Still, I'm here to kick off my staycation and I want a treat. Meaning the cupcake. Not the man who made them. Not really.

Damn.

I push my way through the crowd, and when I arrive at the counter, there it is. A strawberry lemonade cupcake sits next to a cup of coffee. I know he doctored it with the right amount of cream. That's how well he knows me. I look up at him and he gives me an understanding smile.

"Thanks, Ed." I pull out a ten, but he shakes his head.

"I can't charge you for your namesake cupcake."

Yes, he even named a cupcake after me.

Like I said. Ginger. Freaking. Jesus.

"Thank you."

"Your friends are back there," he says pointing over my head.

I glance over my shoulder. EJ and Savannah are sitting at a corner table. They wave me over and I want to go, but I also want to stay near Ed. He smells like sex and vanilla. But definitely not vanilla sex. I'm pretty sure Ed has never had vanilla sex. Of course, I'm thinking about vanilla *and* sex and that leads to me wondering if he uses frosting during sex. If so, what flavor?

Jesus, what is wrong with me?

"Thanks again, Ed," I say, picking up my cupcake and coffee. I make my way over to my friends.

I set my coffee on the table just as EJ jumps up out of her chair and pulls me into a warm embrace. Taller than me by a good five inches, the bookstore owner gives the best hugs. I held my cupcake away from her so not to ruin it but returned the hug with all my might using my free arm.

She pulls back and smiles at me. EJ always seems larger than life. Not because she is curvy. She has that kind of personality. Funny, warm, EJ is beautiful both in spirit and body. She dresses like a bohemian and talks faster than I thought humanly possible, unless you were a character on the Gilmore Girls. With her deep Georgia accent, it is sometimes difficult to understand her. Today, she's wearing her red hair down, the curls spilling over her shoulders.

"Doing okay?" she asks.

I nod. Savannah smiles up at me. "Sit down before you collapse. I think you need some sugar."

"Gee, you're so warm and inviting."

My other best friend snorts and flips me off. Savannah Martinez, the youngest and most talented of the Martinez Restaurant family. While EJ is open and boisterous, Savannah is pessimistic and quiet. I'm truly touched that she is here after closing the night before. Saturday mornings are for sleeping in Savannah's world.

"Be nice or I won't treat you to your favorite tonight."

My mouth waters. "Cheese enchiladas?"

"Yeah. And I took tonight off, which is a big thing."

And it is. Savannah is the head chef for her family's most successful restaurant. Taking a Saturday night off is not a normal thing, especially the weekend before Cinco de Mayo. Their restaurant will definitely be packed with idiots.

"Thank you."

"I think we should go to La Trinidad," Savannah says. Her family owns the restaurant, and while Savannah oversees all their restaurants, La Trinidad is the one she works in. "We can drink Austin's margaritas, then make him drive us home."

Savannah's oldest brother makes the best margaritas.

"That sounds like a plan."

"What are you three planning?" my brother Harry asks as he leans down and kisses the top of my head. He's four years older, but we're closer than most other siblings I know. It came from what we endured together as children while our mother was sick. That fear never really leaves you after one of your parents fights for their life.

He's wearing trousers and a white shirt, his custom uniform. There's no reason to dress so nice since all he does is handle the books for Camos and Cupcakes, but Harry likes to dress like he has a real job. His words, not mine. I know. He's kind of anal, but I still love him. Most of the time.

"I'm going to eat my cupcake, then we are going to go out tonight for dinner. I take it after EJ gets done with the shop?" I raise one eyebrow in question.

EJ nods. "Yeah. Sammy's closing tonight."

"You're going to leave her on her own?" I ask. Sammy is a sweet college student, but she has the air of absent-minded professor about her.

"Naw. I hired another pretty boy. He'll keep her company."

"Do you always use derogatory terms for men like that?" My brother asks without malice.

"It's not. He is pretty and he's twenty, so he *is* a boy. And he's good at work."

"So, you're going out too, Savannah?" he asks.

"Yeah," she says, looking down at her phone with a frown. She's not being rude, she's being Savannah. Her family's business makes it impossible for her to ever get away. There are constant texts and emails and while my job as a chemo nurse can kick my ass, I don't think I would ever be able to deal with Savannah's life.

"I've been promised cheese enchiladas and Austin Margaritas."

They weren't a thing but that's what I call them. I am going to drink my weight in them since I won't have Ed's frosting to eat. And, of course, that leads to other thoughts and euphuisms. I really do need to find a man.

"So, no guys?" he asks.

"No. Absolutely not. We want no men horning in on our fun."

"What about Austin?" he asks.

"He doesn't count," I say.

"I think he might disagree with you," Savannah says, humor lacing her words.

"You know what I mean. He's our margarita man. MM." I like that acronym. I think we need to start calling him that.

"Well, make sure you call me if you three need a ride home," he says. I might be almost thirty, but my brother still sees me as a tween who needs to check in.

"Thank you. Now, go away. I'm sure you have numbers to crunch."

He laughs and leaves us to our cupcakes.

"I have no idea why he puts up with you," Savannah says.

"He *has* too. We're blood. Plus, I'm still holding the goods on a few stories that can be used as blackmail. I know it. He knows it."

I slip my finger over the icing lightly, just skimming a little of the sugary sweetness off the top. I lick my finger and bite back a hum. Barely. The fresh strawberry frosting is light and sweet and...damn. Just that little taste has my head thinking of all kinds of bad things. I imagine that he made this cupcake in particular for me—wearing nothing but an apron.

"You're both adults. I have a feeling that blackmail time is past," EJ says.

"You have no siblings, so you have no idea. Tell her, Savannah."

Savannah pulls her attention back from ger phone and looks at me, then EJ. "She's probably right. Plus, Harry is so OCD it'll drive him crazy not to tie up all those loose ends."

"What the hell does that mean?" EJ asks. She truly has no idea what we're talking about.

"There's this thing between siblings. It's primal. We all fight for attention from our parents until they die. Knowing my brothers and sister, they would probably even figure out a way to get back at me after my parents leave earth," Savannah says.

"And, let's be honest. Part of the fun is leaving Harry wondering what I have on him."

"He doesn't know?" EJ asks.

I shake my head as I slowly pull the paper from my cupcake. I like to take my time whenever I eat an Ed cupcake. Part of it is because I don't eat many of them, because I'd weigh six hundred pounds if I consumed as many of them as I truly wanted. But the other reason, the most important reason of all, is because Ed made them, and that makes them the best cupcakes in the world. Also, there was a little tiny part of me that hoped he was thinking about me when he made them. Even better if he baked them while naked.

My eyes slide closed as I bite into the little treat and moan. The tart lemon, with a hint of sour cream, along with the super sweet strawberry frosting, danced over my taste buds.

"Good lord, get a room," EJ says.

My eyes pop open and I realize that both of my friends are watching me. I swallow, then reach for my coffee.

"What?"

"You sound like you're having sex with your cupcake," Savannah says. "Just ask him out already."

I sniff. "I have no idea what you're talking about."

"Sweetie, please, we know you're still in love with Ed," EJ says.

My face heats. "I'm not in love with him."

Sure, I told them more than once about my crush, but there's no reason for my friends to know that I am neck deep in love and going under for the third time. Or that I think a lot about his...frosting.

"It's the cupcake and that's it."

I glare them both into silence, then pick up my cupcake and start to eat it again. Nothing is going to dampen my experience with my treat.

Chapter Two

Ed

As I watch Allison take another bite of her cupcake, I almost pass out. My head spins as all the blood seemingly drains out of it and travels south. Jesus, this is embarrassing, but I can't stop watching her. Her enjoyment of the cupcake I made for her borders on the erotic. I know she doesn't think that way, but I do. I can't help it. It's my heaven and hell each time she devours one of my cupcakes.

She smiles at something her friend EJ says, and I feel my lips curve in response. Allison has the best smile in the world. It's warm enough to make me want to pull her into a big bear hug. Then strip her down and lick every bit of flesh on her body.

I shift my feet trying to ease the pressure in my pants. It does nothing but rub the zipper of my jeans against my dick. That friction makes my arousal even worse. Every day, I try to convince myself that she won't have this effect on me. I give myself a pep talk before she shows up. It's all completely useless.

Every. Fucking. Time.

No matter how many times I tell myself she's not for me, I forget all those rules the moment I see her. She's a sweet woman. She's my best friend's little sister. Definitely off limits. Worse, the first time I met her, she was barely past puberty and was still all gangly and unsure of herself. She was a nuisance I put up with because she was sweet even back then.

Now, she's definitely past that. Hell, she's so damned sure of herself. That's sexier on a woman than lingerie.

The second bite she takes sends another wave of heat coursing through my body. Jesus Fucking Christ. This is...

I take a long breath and try to get my dick under control once again. There are a number of kids in the shop since it's Saturday. Walking around with a hard-on might cause a scene. Besides, she has no idea that I lust after her every damned day. I know I'm not the kind of guy she goes for and, because I am a sick bastard, that makes me want her more. I want her to look at me like she looks at the cupcakes I make for her.

When I first met her, she had a ton of frizzy hair and braces. Now, that hair is chin length, soft and straight, except for that curve at the very end of her tresses. Her eyes have always been sexy, the color of a green moss. Her emotions are easy to read, even now that she's almost thirty years old. Nowadays, she does something cute with her eye makeup that draws them up, reminding me of a cat. And there is one thing you could count on is she showed her emotions in them. I always know what she's thinking about in any situation just by looking at her eyes. EJ makes a comment and Allison frowns. Damn, I even find that sexy. Mainly because I want to kiss the frown away, then trail kisses down her body so I can bury my face between her legs and taste her sweet pussy.

"Hey, how's it going today?" Harry asks as he claps me on the shoulder, ripping me from the very pleasant fantasy of seducing Allison. His sister.

Fuck. Nothing like having my best friend intrude on my mental stalking of his sister. It's something that shames me on a daily basis, but I can't seem to resist her lure. I am definitely going to hell.

"Doing okay. Already ran out of the snickerdoodle."

"Not that I need any, but damn. What's a guy got to do to have his favorite cupcake on hand when he walks in?" he asks.

"Pay me more?" I say as I force myself to turn around. I think I have myself under control, but I know watching Allison any more won't help me stay that way. Standing there drooling and fighting my growing erection isn't a good idea, especially with Harry in front of me.

Harry looks like his sister to a certain degree. He's got brown hair and green eyes. That's about where it stops. Harry's over six feet tall and big like a linebacker. When he said he would grow a beard, Fritz and I thought he wouldn't be able to let it go. But he'd grown a beard, and while it was as long as mine, it seemed like he kept it trimmed better than I do. Knowing Harry, he trims it every day. He's one of the best friends a guy like me could hope for, which makes me lusting after Allison even worse.

"How long has my sister been here?"

"Just a few minutes."

"I figured since she just started in on that cupcake. It usually takes less than three minutes from the time she gets a cupcake until it disappears. They're going out tonight."

"They?" Dammit. I didn't know she was dating again. I try to control my jealousy, but I fail. It's not as though a woman like Allison would ever go for a guy like me.

"Yeah, Allison and the other two musketeers there," he says, motioning with his hand.

The first thing that hits me is relief, which leaves me almost dizzy. Fuck. As Harry looks back over my shoulder at his sister and her friends, I fight the need to turn around. I shouldn't look, because if Harry knew what I was thinking every time I looked at his little sister, he would probably kill me. Still, I can't resist. It's an addiction and seeing her is definitely the drug that I covet. I glance over and bite back a groan. She's licking the icing from her fingers. Then she slips one finger into her mouth. As her eyes slide closed, I can't help but imagine her wearing that look of sheer pleasure—and nothing else—as I thrust my cock between those two very plump lips. Good God, that should be illegal in public. Just watching her has every hormone in my body standing at attention and ready to attack.

My cock swells, the hum of arousal beats through my

blood. I want to taste her. Her mouth, her flesh...I want to bury my face between her legs and make her come.

"Which means I'll have to be on call even though I've got a date," Harry says, pulling my attention away from his sister. I take a second to make sure I can even speak.

I close my eyes and thank the gods I have an apron on. Hopefully, her brother hadn't noticed my erection. When I open my eyes, I find him frowning. "Why? They're grown women."

He rolls his eyes and starts rearranging things on the counter. Harry can't stand to have things off even just an inch. Lately, he's been getting worse. "Who always calls me when they need a driver?"

"Because you tell them to call. Man, you have got to take a step back."

It's something we talk about on a regular basis. Harry always hovers over those he cares about. Their business—because Fritz and I are his best friends—his sister...everyone. I know the reasons came from their mother's battle with breast cancer when Harry was just sixteen. That makes it even more difficult. Fritz has never had issues like that in his life and, well, I never really had a family. None of my fosters ever made me feel like I belonged. So, Fritz and I can't tell him how to behave. We really don't understand what Harry and Allison have been through. Their mother survived, but I know the ordeal of her treatment had affected both siblings.

"Being the call to save the lives of three beautiful women isn't a bad thing."

No one would argue with that. "Hey, why don't you let me take care of it?"

I really don't want to do it, but Harry needs this break. I know it's been months since he's had a date. Not that I can talk, but Harry...he needs to release. Otherwise, he's going to get even more uptight. He's already driving us crazy with his OCD tendencies.

"What are you two talking about?" Fritz asks as he saunters in behind the counter.

The third partner of our business had an interview with a local San Antonio blog about their business. Fritz O'Bryan is the face of our business. He is definitely the prettiest—or at least, that's what Allison says. He has the ability to charm just about any human on earth—especially women. From the ages of five to ninety-five, females seem to fall under his spell. The inky black hair and blue eyes tends to draw them in.

"The three musketeers are going out tonight, and I told them to call if they drink too much."

"Which they will," Fritz says. "Those women can't handle their liquor. And you know, when Savannah starts drinking, she always talks them into tequila. I thought you had a date?"

"I do, but I can cancel."

"No," I say with a little more force than I meant to use. Both Harry and Fritz look at me. I clear my throat. "Listen, you need to go on a date. What if they don't even call you?"

"Yeah?" Harry asks, cocking his head to the side. "You don't have plans tonight?"

I shrug as I lean back against the counter. I rarely have standing plans or go on dates. I'm not that kind of guy. Harry is. At least until the last six months, which made the rest of their lives hell. If he isn't paying attention to a woman, he needles both of us.

"Sure. I was planning on coming in tomorrow to work on some ideas for Fourth of July, so I don't have plans. You need to go out on this date. When was your last one?"

"Why is that important?" Harry asks. I know it's his way of trying to deflect the discussion.

"Was it the Date From Hell?" I ask. The Date From Hell is the title of his one time on a date with EJ. Allison had set them up and it had not gone well at all. In fact, the ladies had an acronym for it: DFH. They all knew what it meant and I'm pretty sure Harry does too.

"Oh, boy, you're right," Fritz says with a chuckle.

"I've been on other dates since then."

"What are you three jabronies talking about?" Allison asks from behind me.

I jump at the sound of her voice. Dammit, she snuck up on us. I can usually control my reaction to her if I prepare. It takes a second too long to turn around, which gets me a knowing look from Fritz.

"Ed said he can be your call tonight," Harry says. I can hear the doubt in his voice, and not because he doesn't trust me. It's because Harry trusts no one but himself.

"Oh?" she says, drawing out the word before making eye contact with me. "We can't fit on your motorcycle."

"I have an SUV also, and you know that," I say crossing my arms over my chest.

"Yeah, and Harry has a date tonight," Fritz says.

Her gaze travels to her brother. "You have a date?"

"He was going to cancel," I offer.

Her eyes widen and right there, I can see the alarm in her green eyes. She knows Harry as well as Fritz and I do. "Oh, no. You go on your date. I said if worse came to worse, we would call an Uber, or Lyft, or whatever."

"Either way, Ed offered since he's going to continue on with his monkish life. Me, I have a date, as usual," Fritz says. Of course, he does. Fritz never met a pretty woman he didn't try to seduce. Except Allison.

She turns her attention to me. I feel it all the way to the soles of my feet. How can one glance almost make me come? "Is that so?"

"No plans tonight."

"What? You have no plans for a Saturday night?"

I don't know why people seem to think I have a lot of dates. Or hookups, or whatever. I haven't had a woman in a really long time. And by long time, I mean we've been through an entire season of every sport since I had a hookup. Shut up. I don't have time.

"I'm coming in tomorrow to test out some new recipes."

She gasps, the dramatic sound completely over the top and I can't help but smile. She smacks me on the arm and even that brief contact arouses me. It makes me want to grab her by the lapels of her red shirt and yank her closer for a kiss. And a whole lot more. A. Lot. More.

"And you didn't tell me?" she asks, her voice filled with horror and mock anger.

"Now you're in trouble," Fritz mumbles.

"It's new recipes, as in you don't have any idea if they'll be good."

She narrows her eyes and crosses her arms beneath her breasts. It plumps them up a bit over the edge of her bodice. It takes all of my control not to slip my finger over the mounds of flesh...or my tongue. My tongue would be good.

"If you make it, then they will be good."

"That means I don't need a taste tester."

She purses her lips, a sure sign that she's pissed. Most men wouldn't find it attractive. I'm not most men.

"I better get a text."

I roll my eyes. "Okay."

"Either way, I doubt we'll be calling you tonight. We're going to Savannah's restaurant, so if we need a ride, someone in her family will take care of us."

"Just remember to call if you need me," I say.

I watch as something comes and goes in her gaze, her expression turning neutral. For the first time since I've known her, I don't know exactly what that look meant.

"Come on," EJ yells out.

Allison rolls her eyes and smiles. "My friends are delicate flowers."

"Allison," Harry says with a warning tone.

"I promise to call Ed if we need him."

"Thank you."

"Have fun and use protection, Harry," she says as she scurries away.

"Yeah, Harry," Fritz says as he settles his arm over Harry's shoulders. "Since it's been so long, a lot of your condoms are probably out of date."

"Get bent," Harry says, pushing Fritz away.

"Who is it?" Fritz asks.

"One of my old clients. Tara Adams."

I groan inwardly. This won't work, just like that last woman he dated before the DFH. Harry always picks women who are boring. Tara Adams is boring. Beyond boring.

"I don't remember her," Fritz remarks.

And that says it all. If Fritz forgot a pretty woman, she has to be damned boring. Hell, any woman. Fritz is the kind of guy who can flirt with just about any woman and make her think she's special. It's why he's our spokesperson.

"She runs that dress shop down on Barbe Street."

The King William district in San Antonio is a small but thriving area and, for the most part, everyone knows everyone else. While we were trying to get our business up and running a couple years ago, Harry did a lot of bookkeeping for the area businesses. Tara is one of those people. One of those very boring people. Talking to her was a bit like watching paint dry.

"What's wrong?" Harry asks me.

"What?"

"You're frowning. What?"

I shake my head. "Nothing."

"No. Not nothing. There's something you want to say."

I want to ignore the question but cannot. "You need a different kind of woman."

"Who is this woman?" Fritz asks again.

"Black hair, blue eyes, has tons of trinkets in her shop," I say.

"She doesn't have a restaurant?" he asks.

Harry shoves his hands through his hair. "Jesus, Fritz, I just said it was a dress shop."

"She was here two days ago, and she was talking to Harry. I thought you were doing her books again."

Harry shook his head. "Only ours these days, thank God."

"Oh..." Fritz says, then he looks at Harry. "Yeah, she's not right for you."

"We have similar tastes," Harry says with a frown.

I know that if we rag on him too much, he'll cancel the date. Even if the sex sucks—and not in a good way—it's better he gets out.

"You do. And now that you don't have to worry about your sister and her friends, you can go out and have fun tonight."

He nods. "Exactly. Anyway, I need to go over a few things on our books unless you need me out here."

I shake my head. "If we get a rush, Fritz and I can handle it. I'm done with baking for the day."

He nods and heads back to the office.

"What the hell did you do that for?" Fritz asks the minute Harry is out of earshot. "She's so wrong for him."

"He needs a break and to let off some steam."

He groans. "That woman is so boring. I remember her now. When we did the grand opening, she refused to eat anything, even the fruit. It wasn't on her diet plan. She's just like him."

I shrug. "Do you want him to get off, or do you want him to continue to wind himself up into a tight ball?"

Fritz opens his mouth, then snaps it shut. "Okay, you have a point."

"I'm usually right."

"Get bent, Cooper."

I chuckle.

"When are you going out on a date?"

I shrug. "Not sure."

"Why aren't you as wound up as Harry?"

"I don't have dates. I have hookups and that works just fine for me." Which is somewhat true. Okay, I haven't been out in months and months...and well, fuck. It's not important.

"One of these days you might want more," he warns.

"I'll worry about that when I come to that bridge."

He nods. His attention turns to a customer who just walked up, leaving me to my thoughts. There is no worry about dates or happily ever after. I'm not built for them. There is only one person who tempts me, and Allison is off limits. Besides, she isn't the least bit interested in me.

Maybe one day, I can get my body to catch up with that fact.

Chapter Three

Allison

The moment I step into La Trinidad, my mouth starts watering. I ate lightly all day to prepare for my inevitable evening of overeating. Well, after I devoured my cupcake this morning, that is. I almost went back for a second one, because I know Ed would keep an extra one behind the counter for me. Again. Ginger Jesus. Hmm...wait, no. No thinking about him tonight.

I draw in a deep breath, as the scent of Mexican spices surround me. God, I love living in south Texas, especially San Antonio. Tex Mex is my favorite kind of food, and there is no shortage of good restaurants to choose from. Although, we do seem to end up at La Trinidad most nights. One thing is for sure: I'm going to eat all the enchiladas and drink all the margaritas I possibly can.

"Earth to Allison," EJ says, snapping her fingers in front of my face.

I blink, then focus on her. "Sorry. I was thinking that I'm ready to eat. And drink. Drink a lot. And eat a lot."

She laughs and I notice heads turning. It was like that all the time when we went out. EJ's happy spirit always attracts people. Whether she's laughing, speaking, or just walking through a room, heads turn. It's like she is a bohemian fairy who can attract anyone within a five-block radius. Tonight is no exception. The maxi dress hugs her ample chest, and the greens in the flowery design go perfectly with her red hair and green eyes.

"It's been a long time since we've gone out," she says. "Savannah has our favorite booth."

It's the one closest to the bar, and that's what tonight is all about for Savannah. Her life revolves around the restaurant and her family business. She has very little personal time, so when she does, she lets loose. I have a feeling there is an Uber in our future.

She's sitting in the booth already. It's one of those u-shaped deals, so EJ takes one side and I take the other.

"I assumed you would both want margaritas, and I put in our orders already." She'd texted us about an hour earlier asking what we wanted. We've both been to the restaurant so many times, we know the menu by heart.

She has her own margarita and it's almost gone. The two glasses sitting on the table have been ordered perfectly. Mango for EJ and strawberry for me—of course.

The first sip is gloriously sweet and tart. Austin made them with us in mind, so it's strong. Damn, it's good.

"Oh, God, I needed this," I say. I smack my lips.

"Strawberry, hmm." I shimmy a bit in happiness. There is enough tequila to add a sting to the sweetness.

"So, the strawberry cupcake didn't do it for you?" Savannah asks as she wiggles her eyebrows.

"It's strawberry lemonade, which you should call it the Allison, since that's what it's called by all the best people."

Of course, that had not been her question. From their amused looks, both my friends know I am trying to avoid the subject.

"I will not allow one enchilada to be served, let alone queso, if you do not at least admit that you're still infatuated with Ed Cooper."

When Savannah drinks, her voice carries. Seeing that she has had at least one margarita already, her voice is starting to rise in volume.

"Shhh," I say as I look around.

EJ and Savannah share a smile, and I realize how stupid I sound. Sure, people know Camos and Cupcakes, but they don't know me. I'm sure there are a lot of women who talk about being infatuated with Ed. He's that kind of guy. A bad boy with a touch of sweetness. That kind of man attracts women. I've seen them at the shop, more than once.

Great, now I'm depressed. I need to shove those thoughts aside and think about my staycation and the celebration tonight.

"Fine, I *am* but in a purely basic way. You know. Cuz of the cupcakes."

EJ lets one perfectly sculpted eyebrow rise.

"That's such bullshit, Strawberry Lemonade," Savannah says, using my cupcake as my name. She does that when she is feeling feisty and after a few margaritas. That one thought has me wondering just how many drinks she's consumed.

I frown at her. "I said to quit calling me that."

She smirks at me and sips up the rest of her margarita with noisy slurps. La Trinidad is large, with ceramic floors and music playing. Still, the sound of her slurping is so loud, it attracts the attention of a few people. She ignores them because Savannah doesn't give a damn what people think. At least, outside of her family.

"Ladies," Austin says, standing next to the table. "Do we need another refill?"

I squint up at Savannah's older brother. He's pretty, that's for sure, but definitely not my type. First of all, he's pretty. I think Ed is gorgeous, but it's because he isn't really pretty. Also, Austin is like a brother to me. Savannah, Austin, and I were all in high school at the same time, and he irritates me about as much as my own brother does. But he *is* pretty with his wavy black hair and golden eyes. He can also make the best margaritas so that's a plus.

"Yes," Savannah says, slamming her glass back down on the table so hard I'm amazed she didn't break it.

"Maybe you should let these two catch up with you," he suggests.

Savannah's eyes narrow and I can see there is a fight brewing. Savannah might seem cool and collected when she's sober—which is most of the time—but when she drinks, she's always raring for a fight. When it's a family member, she likes the fight even more.

"I think you need to mind your own fucking business." Oh, not good. Savannah cusses with the best of us, but with that tone, it definitely means we might have a bad night. Or maybe, a good night. Sometimes, it's fun to let Savannah be drunk Savannah.

EJ giggles and I shake my head.

"You know this will just end badly for you. It's like when she broke your nose," I say, trying my best to be helpful.

"Which time?" he asks with a laugh.

"All of them. I'll make sure to keep her in check," I say as I offer a smile.

"I have no idea why you are friends with my sister. You're definitely too sweet." He gives me a sexy smile, or at least, I'm sure a lot of women find it sexy. Me, I see a guy who was just as sweet in high school as he is now. And I know for a fact that he thinks of me as a sister.

"Back off, Austin. Strawberry Lemonade is spoken for," Savannah says as she hiccups.

"Also, maybe get our food here as fast as possible, or some queso?" I ask. He nods and grabs his sister's empty glass.

After he leaves, I look at Savannah and snort. She's got one eye closed as she studies me. "You don't have the hots for Austin, do you? He's not your type."

Just because I was thinking the same thing a minute earlier doesn't mean... "What's that supposed to mean? Austin's a sweetie."

"Exactly. You're both too damn nice. It would be like polite chipmunks dating." She sits up straighter and mimics the voice of the chipmunks. "After you. Oh, no, after you."

"So you think I need someone mean?"

I look at EJ, who shrugs. Truth is, Savannah hardly ever drinks, so she doesn't have the resistance to it that we do. Also, she weighs almost next to nothing.

"No. Not mean. Only...you need a yang."

I blink. As a nurse, I might not be completely naive, but there are some sexual terms I don't know. "A what?"

She sighs so loud and dramatically, I fight a smile. I'm afraid if I do smile, she'll get pissed and I could be the one with the broken nose.

"You're the yin. You need a yang. I think Ed Cooper is your yang."

"He thinks of me as his little sister."

She snorts. "Nope. I don't think so."

"What do you mean?"

I look at EJ when Savannah doesn't answer. EJ smiles at me. "Well, you know, he did name a cupcake after you."

"Strawberry Lemonade!" Savannah shouts drawing more attention to them.

"What does that have to do with anything?" I ask.

"He hasn't named any cupcakes after me and I'm there every single day for coffee," EJ points out. "And you haven't seen the way he looks at you."

I scoff at that but EJ shakes her head.

"Listen, I could be wrong, but you know I am rarely wrong."

"Yet you're so modest," Savannah says.

EJ ignores her. "You don't see the way he looks at you when you aren't looking."

"How does he look at me?" I ask, almost afraid of the answer.

"Like you're the only person in the world."

"Stars in his eyes," Savannah says, smacking her lips.

I look between the two of them, then snort.

"You two need help."

"No, I need some foods."

"Foods?" I ask Savannah. She's a little more out of control than she normally is. "Is that a chef term?"

"Yes," then she claps when her brother sets down their drinks.

"Get lost, boss," someone says from behind him. A curvy blonde waitress smiles as he steps aside. She has queso, more chips, and some quesadillas. My stomach growls loudly, though the music covers the sound. I knew I was hungry, but I had no idea.

"I have your orders in now, so you have time to eat this before your dinners show up," the waitress says.

"Thank you," I say with a smile.

"Anything for Savannah." She looks at her. "Make sure you eat."

Then she disappears. "She's kind of bossy," Savannah says, grabbing one of the quesadillas. "But she's the best damned waitress."

I nod, remembering the few times she's waited on me.

The moment I slipped the cheese covered chip into my mouth, I close my eyes and hum. God, I needed this... needed time out with my friends.

"So, SL—get it?—what are you going to do about Ed?" Savannah asks.

What can I do? The truth is, I have no idea. I've had a crush on him, and he sees me as his little sister. I need to do something about it, find some man to get him off my mind. Not like I haven't been with men or had relationships.

"Nothing. Man doesn't want a relationship with me."

"Fuck a relationship. Get some sex," she says, louder again. A few people turn and look at us, and I try my best not to shush her. That will only make her louder.

I lean closer. "Funny comments coming from the one virgin in the group."

She snorts. "I live vicariously through both of you, at least until lately. I mean, give a girl some help here."

"I did. I gave you a gift certificate to that sex toy shop," EJ says.

"Oh, yeah ya did," Savannah says as she clinks her margarita glass with EJ's. "You agree with me, though, right?"

EJ looks at me. "Yeah, she needs to *do* Ed Cooper. Like a lot. Like all night long."

Even a little tipsy, I can't fight the blush. It is the fate of being so fair skinned. There is nothing I would like more. Well, first there would be world peace, a cure for cancer, then doing Ed Cooper. Yeah. That's what I want to do.

"Ohh, that look," EJ says with a giggle. "I would love to know what was behind it."

"Probably thinking about Edward," Savannah says making kissy noises in my direction.

"He's not interested, so maybe we can think about someone else I should do."

"I think you're insane, but okay. We'll play along," EJ says. "What about Austin?"

"Oh, gross. I wouldn't want to date Austin," Savannah says making gagging noises.

"He's your brother. Of course, you don't want to date him. I've always thought he was very sexy," EJ says.

I glance up at Austin, who is behind the bar keeping one eye on his customers and one eye on us. He is attractive, but he's too much of a friend. Kind of like Harry.

"Is he the reason you termed the one date you went on with Harry as The Date from Hell? You would rather go out with Austin?"

I made the mistake of fixing them up. Harry and EJ should have a lot in common, but for some reason, they rubbed each other the wrong way. She said he was enough to put her off of dating and that's saying a lot. EJ dates a great deal.

"No. Your brother is the reason it was the DFH."

I cock my head to the side and study her. There's something odd there. "What?"

She sighs. "Your brother is very controlling. You know I don't like that. So, Austin is out. Who else? Oh, what about that paramedic...Todd?"

"Trent?"

"Yeah. What about him?"

It's hard to admit that I forgot I went out on a date with him. In fact, I remember a text about a month or two ago.

"We have got to get you laid and get Ed off your brain," Savannah says.

"Look who's talking," I say, eyeing Savannah. She's the only virgin out of the three of us. She isn't particularly saving herself, she just always said she hadn't met a guy worth the trouble when batteries did the trick.

"Besides, it's not like she hasn't had sex," EJ says.

Of course, Austin picks that moment to step up to the table. He studies all of us. "Please tell me that you're not talking about my sister."

"No. We're talking about Strawberry Lemonade," Savannah says.

"Who?"

"Me."

"Oh, well..."

The look on his face has me dissolving into giggles. "Don't worry. You're not in the running."

"Get out of here, loser," Savannah says.

"Hey, take it easy and keep it down," he says, watching his sister closely. Out of the five siblings, he and Savannah are the closest. And he looks genuinely worried about her. I make a mental note to call him next week to see what's up. I just hope I remember it after tonight, because there is a good chance I won't remember a lot of it later.

"We'll keep it together, Austin," I say.

"Yes," EJ says smiling up at him and sucking on her straw.

There is a long moment where Austin watches her like he wanted her to be the one looking for sex. He tears his gaze away from EJ to look at his sister again.

"Just remember, everyone here knows who you are."

Then he turns to go back to the bar, but not before smiling at EJ.

"Whoa, hot man alert." She fans herself dramatically with her hand.

I giggle. Not a normal thing for me, but the margarita is starting to go to my head, which is starting to feel kind of floaty.

"Ugh, please, stop that," Savannah says, disgust evident in her tone and on her face.

"Sorry," EJ says, tossing a red curl over her shoulder. "Your brother is hot. Right, Allison?"

Savannah looks at me, her eyes narrowing, and I shrug. "Sorry, but he is. If I didn't think of him like a brother, I'd say he was fuckable."

"See," EJ says.

Savannah holds her hands over her ears. "Stop it. My virgin ears can't handle the fucking "f" word."

Again, I start giggling just as the food arrives. The same waitress appears with our orders.

She waits until another waiter sets up one of those stands, then she sets the large tray on top of it.

"Well, here is some food to soak up that alcohol," she says, picking up a platter of cheese enchiladas. She sets it in front of me. Then she gives EJ her shrimp fajitas, and

Savannah her carne asada. "I'll be back with more chips."

She whisks away the serving platter and stand.

"Best waitress," Savannah says again. "I really don't know what we would do without her."

One thing I love about my friends is that they are always supportive of anyone in the service industry. I've worked with the public, but I'm a little more specialized now. Still, I have an appreciation for just how hard it is to deal with the public at large and, of course, Savannah and EJ still work in it.

We dig into our meals and, as expected, the food is amazing. The restaurant regularly wins awards and is voted one of the best for Tex Mex cuisine in San Antonio on a lot of travel and food blogs. All of it has to do with Savannah. She's been running the restaurant since she was twenty-two.

"So, we need to find you someone, Strawberry Lemonade."

I want to tell her to stop calling me that name, but I know it will do no good. "I've been looking, just, it's hard when you work in a profession like I do. The only cutie we have in the infusion center is gay."

"No sexy doctors?" EJ asks. I make a face. They both know I want nothing to do with doctors. "Okay, then, maybe we should hit the clubs or go down to the River Walk this week."

I roll my eyes. "The River Walk, really? I don't want to pick up tourists."

"Why not?" EJ asks. "They are the perfect pick me up. No strings, no worries."

I've never been into casual sex. I don't find anything wrong with it, or with EJ's view on it. But I do have an issue with it. I cannot fall into bed with a guy unless I'm emotionally attached.

"Oh, right. See, that's your problem. Maybe you need a little house cleaning. You don't want to end up like Savannah."

That's true, although, the stress she deals with makes it hard for her to even date at times. Savannah's family business hinges on her ability to keep all the balls in the air. It's a lot for anyone to handle, let alone a twenty-eight-year-old.

"Okay. Maybe. We could go out early in the week," I say. "That works better for you, right, Savannah?"

She nods a she shovels food into her mouth. I'm thankful she's at least eating.

Austin arrives back at our table. "Here you go, ladies...and Savannah."

She scowls her brother but says nothing as she continues to eat.

"Thanks, Austin," EJ says smiling at him. He grins back at her, and I wonder at these two. Both of them are alike in many ways. They attract the opposite sex on a regular basis, and I have noticed that Austin tends to date taller more voluptuous women like her.

"Let me know if you need anything," Austin says before leaving us to our drinks and food.

"Damn, that man has the best smile."

"Nope," Savannah says as she dips a chip into the queso.

"What?" EJ asks.

"I was just explaining to Strawberry Lemonade here that she shouldn't date nice people. She needs a yang and so do you."

EJ looks at me. "Please explain to me why the virgin thinks she should be giving us advice."

I smile. "She might be right. You are both kind of doggy when he comes to the opposite sex."

Savannah snorts but says nothing as she picks up her fresh margarita.

"Doggy?" EJ asks.

I shrug. "You're both bright stars and attract a lot of attention. You probably need someone a little different from you."

"There you go. Yang," Savannah says.

"And besides, tonight is about us and not men. Let's do girls' night right," I say holding up my glass. "To us."

"Yes," Savannah says holding up her glass. EJ smiles and does the same.

"May we not remember some of the embarrassing things we say," I say.

We clink our glasses together. As I sip my margarita, I remind myself that this is the kick off to my staycation and worrying about Ed is just a waste of my time.

Chapter Four

Ed

It's just past nine o'clock on a Saturday night, and I can feel my body wanting to give in to sleep. The Rangers are on, but I'm barely paying attention. Instead, I feel my entire body screaming for me to head back to bed. Before ten o'clock on a weekend night. What the fuck has become of me? I know what's become of me. The damned shop. The one I love all of the time and hate some of the time. Fritz and Harry give me shit, but they aren't the ones who are keeping baker's hours, up at three in the morning to make sure I have time to get everything ready before we open at six.

At least I finally have a part-timer. I haven't had time off in the eighteen months since we opened, other than holidays and my Sundays and Mondays. There has been no one else to handle the baking. It's thanks to EJ, who told Harry they were abusing me, that I have any help. Thanks to Allison's friend, I was going to be able to have my first three days off in eighteen months.

And, just like that, I'm thinking about Allison. Sure, I used a roundabout way, but don't judge me lest you be judged, or some shit like that. Granted, the woman is on my brain too much. I want her in a way that is a little scary, and it is getting worse by the day. I know part of the reason is because I have been a monk lately. But every time I think about going out, or meeting an attractive woman at the shop, Allison's face pops up in my mind. And those plump lips, that curvy little body...fuck.

I groan as my dick twitches. She thinks of me as a brother, and here I'm thinking about how good it would feel to slide into her tight, wet pussy. I close my eyes attempting to gain some self-control, but it does no good. I get a flash of her naked in my bed, her legs spread, her pretty little cunt dripping with need.

Fuck me. Not a very brotherly thing to do. It's another indication that I'm no good for her.

I come from nothing. Less than nothing. My mother was an addict who abandoned me. I have no fucking idea who my father was. I bounced around from foster home to foster home, until I aged out and entered the Army. That was a godsend. Before I entered, I was on a one-way track to disaster. Drinking, smoking a little weed, definitely getting in fights. The Army gave me discipline, a purpose. Along the way, I picked up two of the best friends a guy could ask for and found out I make the best fucking cupcakes a man could ever hope to make.

I chuckle. The truth is, I would have never seen myself doing this if it wasn't for Fritz and Harry. They were the ones who said we had a chance to make a living without putting our lives on the line. I kind of liked that idea. The Army was offering some bonuses to get out early and all three of us decided to do just that. Being in business with them is better than I could have hoped for. Two years after we came up with the idea, and eighteen months after we opened, we're considered one of the best up and coming bakeries in San Antonio. We get regular write ups in statewide and national magazines, along with regular mentions on blogs.

So, yeah, I have a good life right now, but I understand that I'm lucky to have it. Fucking it up by taking Allison to bed would be a stupid move.

My phone rings, pulling me out of my thoughts. I grab it up off my end table and see the name. Austin? Why would Savannah's brother be calling me?

"Hey, Austin. What's up?"

"It's the girls."

The girls? Then I remember I'm on call for Allison and her friends.

"They need a ride home?"

"Yeah, they...well, Savannah talked them into shots."

Of course she did. Damn, I owe Fritz twenty bucks.

"Okay, on my way."

"Thanks, man. I called Harry but he was on a date."

"Please tell me he's still on it."

"Yeah, he said if I didn't get hold of you, to call him back."

As if on cue, my call waiting pings. "I'll be there in twenty minutes or so, depending on traffic."

"Thanks again."

I click over to Harry. "Yeah?"

"Did you talk to Austin?"

"Austin who?"

"Don't fuck with me."

I chuckle. "Yep. I'm on my way to round up the *girls*, as Austin called them."

I would never call them that because, well, they were three very sexy women. But I didn't grow up with them.

"Thanks, Ed."

I understand why Harry is the way he is. He was sixteen when his mother had been diagnosed with breast cancer. As close as he and I are, Harry rarely talks of it, but Allison has mentioned that's when his control issues started. I understand that. If I had a mom like Mrs. B, I would freak out too. Hell, I would freak out now, and she's not even my biological mom.

"You still on your date?" I ask.

"Yeah."

I let loose a breath I didn't know I had been holding. "Don't fear, big brother. I'll handle your sister and her friends. Put them out of your thoughts."

"Gotcha. Can you text me?"

Jesus, Harry really needed to learn how to relax. Even though I knew he needed some tough love on his control issues, I wasn't going to rock the boat. "Sure. I'll let you know when I pick her up."

"Great."

Then he hangs up. Harry never wastes time. I scrub a hand over my face, then stand up. My back protests, thanks to an injury on my last deployment. That tells me one thing: rain is coming. Great, I'm officially an old man. I'm predicting the weather because my body is in pain. That's what I get for spending my twenties in service to Uncle Sam.

I shake my head, slip on my shoes, then grab my keys and my wallet. The sooner I got out there, the faster I would get home. Besides, how much of a problem could three sweet women be?

Chapter Five

Allison

Three hours later, I can't feel my face. And, I feel like I'm on one of those swing things at amusement parks. You know, the ones that take you up high and make you fly through the air. The wind shifts through your hair, and you feel like you might fall out of the swing at any minute. Like that. Exactly like that. Also, how many times did I just say feel. A lot.

I know I'm drunk, even though I ate enough for someone twice my size. It should have soaked up some of the two massive margaritas and three...no five!...Tequila shots.

We're all a mess. EJ is getting louder by the moment and Savannah is singing. She only does that when she's plowed, and it's never pretty. In fact, she sounds like a cat being slowly strangled to death.

"Allison," someone says. I turn and almost fall out of the booth. Big hands grab me before I fall on the ground. I look up, then up some more. I know before I see his face that it's Ed. He smells of sugar and cinnamon and sinna-mon. Get it? *Sin*.

"Hey, Ed," I say smiling. "You came out to eat with us?"

His mouth twitches. "Not exactly."

"Thank God," Austin says stepping up beside Ed.

"Thank God for what? For Ed?" I ask. "I say we should thank God for Ed every damn day."

"Here, here!" EJ yells.

I look up at Ed and wonder about his expression. He has kind of fair skin thanks to that red hair, and his face turns a little pinker than usual. Ed Cooper is blushing? And just how far does that go down? Like is his chest pink from blushing?

"I have this one," he says to Austin.

Austin nods. "I can handle the other two. They live five minutes from each other."

"Come on, Allison."

"Nope."

There is a beat of silence. When he speaks, his voice isn't as amused.

"Excuse me?" he asks.

I close one eye and look at him. There is a tone in his voice that would probably make most people run in the opposite direction. But I am not most people. I'm Straw-berry Lemonade.

"What do you mean you're strawberry lemonade?" he asks.

EJ and Savannah dissolve into giggles.

He glances at them, but then his gaze comes back to

me and I feel like I won the lottery. People look at the big bear of a man and think he's some kind of hard ass. He is, in a lot of ways. But there is this gooey center I want to reach. Not on the level I can now. The friend's sister, the one who cannot be anything but a sweet irritation. I want to be the woman who brings him to his knees.

He snaps his fingers in front of my face. I frown and bat his hand away.

"Stop that. Having a fantasy."

He rolls his eyes. "Come on, Allison. I told Harry I'd take care of you tonight."

"Awe," EJ and Savannah say together.

I turn and say, "Isn't he the sweetest?"

Apparently, Ed has had enough of my antics. He grabs my hand, tugging me out of the booth. Then, like I weigh nothing at all, he picks me up in his arms.

"Ed," I say as my face heats. "I can walk."

"I asked you to leave. You didn't." His tone of voice tells me he doesn't find this funny at all.

He turns to leave but EJ calls out to him. She's the bestest friend, saving me from the uber sexiness of Ed. Being carried out like this is too romantic, and I can't resist the man now. Not that he is doing anything other than dragging his best friend's drunk sister out of the restaurant.

"Stop!"

He sighs and turns back. That's when I see her holding up my purse.

"She needs this."

She slips out of the booth and hands it to me. "I thought you were saving me from embarrassment."

EJ laughs and says, "Just helping you get your yang."

"That's it?" he asks.

"Yeah, we know she's safe with you."

He nods and then turns to leave. This time he takes me past giggling patrons and waitstaff out into the sultry Texas night. Once we get to his SUV, he sets me down on my feet and I sigh. Being pressed up against him is the best thing ever. I'm completely surrounded by his scent, that sugary sweetness along with his own masculine scent. I just want to lick him up and down. Like start at the top and go all the way down to the bottom, spending most of the time in the middle because that's the interesting parts. Like his mouth and that amazing butt. And the dangly bits. Plus, he's all hard and warm.

"Allison," he says, his voice strangled.

"What?"

"You're killing me here. Why are you thinking I'm hard and warm?"

"Did I say that?"

He looks down at me. It's dark in the parking lot, but not that dark. I can see his beautiful blue gaze watching me. They aren't completely blue actually. There's more grey than blue in his right eye, and it has always intrigued me. Then, I let my gaze drop to his mouth. I know it's wicked. I know a man like Ed could make me come wit that sinful mouth.

"Allison," his says, his voice just above a whisper.

"Yeah?"

He sighs again—he seems to be doing that a lot tonight—and shakes his head.

Without saying anything, he opens the door and helps me in. My foot slips off the step and I almost fall down. Ed catches me as I giggle. I take a step back and my ass hits his groin as I bend down to grab my purse.

"Allison."

"What?" I'm still giggling.

"Get. In. The. Fucking. Truck."

Then, as if he doesn't trust me to do it, he grabs me by the waist and practically throws me into the passenger seat. He slams the door and stalks around the front of the SUV. He settles in the driver's seat, then looks over at me. There has never been another man so beautiful. He's all beardy and sexy. Wait, is beardy a word?

"Put on your seatbelt," he orders.

"Huh?" I ask, because I'm still trying to figure out if beardy is a word.

Another sigh as he leans across my body and grabs the seatbelt. I can smell him. That sugary scent that seems to cling to him no matter how many showers he takes.

"How many showers do you take a day?"

He growls and doesn't answer my question. Instead, he connects the belt and moves away from me. Which makes me uber sad. Why am I using the word uber so much tonight?

"I don't know."

I look at him. "What?"

"You asked why you were using the word uber so much."

"Oh. I thought I was just thinking that. You know. Thinking thoughts."

His mouth twitches. "Yeah?"

And there it is. The humor. He will always see me as the goofy younger sister of his best friend. I will never attract him in any way, and it irritates me. Life is not fair. I want to be the kind of woman Ed would see as sexy. Why doesn't he? Because I'm boring, that's why.

"Allison?"

"Never mind. Just take me home."

He sighs, the sound loud and obnoxious. When he speaks, he sounds so annoyed. "Now why are you mad?"

"Nothing. No reason. Just...go."

He rolls his shoulders and looks over at me. I don't want him looking at me like I've lost my mind, because there is a good chance I have. Instead, I cross my arms across my chest, lean back in my chair, and close my eyes.

What a great way to start off my staycation.

Chapter Six

Ed

As I drive through the dark streets, there is little traffic. My brain isn't actually running on full power but, thankfully, I can still drive without causing an accident. I shift in my seat as I take the exit off of 1604 that leads to her neighborhood. My cock hasn't settled down since her very ample ass connected with my groin. Of course, I haven't been able to think straight since she held onto me and called me hard and warm. Jesus, the woman was pushing all my buttons tonight. Why, I have no idea. I glance over at her and, from her even breathing, I can tell she's asleep. That apparently is all I need to give me a hard on. Allison...breathing.

I glance over at her again. She has no idea how sexy she is or what kind of power she holds over me. Seriously. For years, I went for women who were a little bit more athletic, and definitely taller than Allison. But, once I moved to San Antonio, I found myself dreaming about her soft curves. I crave a woman who is a little more bottom heavy. I've seen her in jeans and almost walked into a wall when she bent over to pick something up off the ground. It was in the shop, and I almost passed out from the loss of blood in my brain.

I pull up into the driveway of her house and look over. Allison has been asleep for about fifteen minutes now. After getting mad at me for whatever reason, she closed her eyes. It was a needed break from her antics. I know she won't remember any of this, and she didn't mean the things she said about me. It was just the alcohol. Lord knows I won't get any sleep tonight. It's bad enough I've been dating my hand during the last year, but now I will have that memory of her voice. Calling me hard. I glance down at my jean-encased dick. She has no fucking idea how true that statement is. And warm doesn't get close to what I feel.

I draw in a deep breath as I close my eyes and get my mind back on track. I just have to get her into the house and then go home. Easy peasy, right? As I turn off my truck, I look around at the sleepy neighborhood.

She bought her house just a few months ago and since then, she had really made it a home. Her neighbors were mainly retired military and younger families. Of course, she fit in right away. It's quiet already, unlike other parts of San Antonio. It was one of the reasons she bought the house. It took her an extra ten minutes to get to work, but she said that she needed the quiet. Her hours were just as bad as mine.

I look at her and smile. She looks so sweet and peaceful that I hate to wake her up. But I need to get her inside the house. I glance at the door, then back at her. I could carry her in. It makes me a bit of a perv, because when I carried her out of the restaurant, it had been one of the most arousing moments of the last year. Which said so much about me and where my sex life was at the moment.

Shaking those thoughts away, I go to unlock her door. She gave me a key when she bought the house. All three of us, Fritz, Harry and I, were given keys. I'm sure EJ and Savannah each have one as well. After I unlock the door, I jog back to the SUV and open her door.

Reaching across her body, I undo her seatbelt. As I am moving back so I can lift her out of my vehicle, she slips her arms over my shoulders.

"Allison," I say, my voice strained. Her scent surrounds me. It's warm and welcoming and sweet, just like her favorite cupcake.

"Ed," she mumbles. I know she's probably still sleeping, but I can't make myself move away from her. My name on her lips stuns me. "Come here. I want you."

I blink, trying to figure out just how to respond, but it's impossible. My dick is at full staff, and there is no more blood in my brain, so thinking's kind of difficult. In fact, I'm surprised I don't pass out cold.

Before I can react, she pulls me closer to her, pressing her mouth against mine. For a moment I resist, but too many nights dreaming about her has me losing my control and going along for the ride. I feel her tongue trace the seam of my lips and I open to let her dive in. She tastes of tequila and sweet sin. I want her, need her in a way I have never needed another human in my life. I tangle my tongue with hers and she moans, the vibrations filter throughout my entire body. I drink her in, not able to resist this simple pleasure. She pulls back from me and I follow.

"I really want you inside of me, Ed," she says, then promptly passes back out.

For a long moment, I stand there unable to move. My brain has completely drained of all the blood that seems to have taken up permanent residence in my cock.

Fuck me.

Never in my life have I been this turned on. Even during my teenage years where I spent a fair amount of time jacking off, I didn't react this way. Of course, then it had been an abstract idea. Now, there was a hot, sexy woman kissing the fuck out of me. A woman who occupied my mind while I was asleep and awake. I want to wake her up and demand she explain herself. I step away, draw in a huge breath, and count down from ten. I do that four more times before I think I might be able to handle her. I step closer again, then slip my arms beneath her legs and behind her back, lifting her off the seat. Even in sleep, she snuggles up against me, her head on my shoulder and her arms around my neck. I can feel her breath against my skin, and I want to snuggle right back, but I fight that urge. Mostly. It's difficult because I can smell her now. She always seems to smell of sunshine, like I'm laying out in a field, the summer sun beating down on me, the warmth of it on my skin. That's Allison. She's the sunlight in my dark world.

I step into her house, carrying her over the threshold. I pause at the thought, then shake it away. I'm just taking care of my best friend's baby sister. Who isn't a baby in the least. But she should have some of her own. She loves children, and she would be so good at being a mom.

Thinking about her being a mom makes me contemplate just how to give her those babies and I almost drop her. I close my eyes and remind myself of the objective. Get her home, then leave. That's it.

I kick the door shut, then walk through her house all the way back to her room. I hesitate, trying to bolster myself. As I enter her bedroom, I see that massive king bed. I remember it being delivered the day we helped her move in about six months ago. Ever since the moment I saw her jump on it and giggle, I've had fantasies. Well, to be truthful, I've had them since Harry, Fritz, and I got out of the service and moved to San Antonio. The image of her on that bed had intensified them.

I push that thought aside. I'm here to make sure she got home okay. After I place her on top of her bed, I stand there trying to decide if I should take her clothes off, my cock twitches. Damn. Okay, maybe not take off her clothes, but I take off her sandals, then grab a blanket from the chair beside her bed to cover her up with it. There. She's home and safe.

I stand there for a few long moments looking at her. Even in sleep, she has a little smile curving her lips like she's got a secret. The steady rise and fall of her chest tells me she is settled into sleep and there shouldn't be a problem. I linger. I keep finding things in her room to study, as if they hold some kind of secret as to how to get over my embarrassing crush on her. Truthfully, it's a little stalkerish. She mumbles something in her sleep and shifts her weight on the bed. I let go of the breath I am holding, but I can't seem to move. I was just supposed to bring her home. End of story.

Still, I can't get myself to move. I want to slip beneath that blanket, pull her closer, and snuggle. Then I want to strip her clothes off her and fuck her until neither of us can walk.

I can feel a drop of precum leak out and I have to adjust my dick through my clothes. The scrape of my jeans against my cock has me closing my eyes and having to bite back a groan. I would rather her hands were on me. Her hands, her body, her tight cunt. Jesus, I can just imagine the feel of her tightening around me as she comes.

I have to do some counting before I open my eyes, thankful that she's still sleeping.

She doesn't usually drink that much. Maybe I should stay. Just to be sure. I roll my eyes embarrassed for myself. I can't even come up with a decent excuse. Still, I would hate if she got hurt or too sick by herself. Her brother would never forgive me, and I would never forgive myself.

Knowing it's probably stupid, but not able to force myself to leave, I walk out of her bedroom—which takes more than a little control than I thought it would. After I shut her door, I draw in a deep breath, then release it slowly. It's asinine to stay here, but I've never seen

Allison that drunk. Not that she drinks much to begin with.

I push those thoughts aside and go in search of a place to sleep. Her couch is one of those deep ones and is bigger than most, but I know my six-foot four-inch frame is not going to fit on it. I open up one of the other rooms and find an office. I hadn't been back since she moved in no matter how many parties she's had. I forced myself not to be here, near her. I knew I wouldn't be able to avoid her...or that massive king bed she has. Why did she need such a big bed? What the fuck was she planning on doing on it?

I shake my head as I open the door to another spare room and find boxes in it. So, I have the couch or the hard floor. Years ago, I could take the floor, but after my last tour, I can't really deal with that. Well, I could, but I would end up walking like an old man all week.

I walk back to Allison's room. I could sleep next to her. We would both be fully clothed and that way if she needed me in the night, I would be right there. I stand in the doorway, knowing that if I do this, I will have memories of it, which will make it harder for me to even look at her. It was bad enough right now.

I wander over to the right side of the bed. Allison is snuggled up to her pillow, her back to me. She's fully dressed and snoring, and I want to wake her up by slipping my dick into her warm, wet pussy. The woman is sloppy drunk and was being pretty obnoxious just thirty minutes earlier, but even that reminder doesn't get my cock under control. I can do this. I can stay here through the night to make sure she's okay. Harry would expect it of me. I'll sleep on top of the covers with all my clothes on.

After I slip off my shoes, I lay down beside her. I'm on my back staring up at the ceiling, my hands under my head forcing them to behave. Now, if the rest of my body can ignore the pounding in my blood and my hard cock, I'll be fine. There is no doubt I might just go to hell for doing this. I know it has more to do with my need to be near her, but I know this is as far as I can go. She's too good for a man like me, but this single night sleeping beside her fully clothed is better than any hard bout of sex with another woman. I just need to keep my hands off her.

She makes a noise, then rolls over the bed to snuggle up next to me. She slips her arm over my midsection and she settles her head on my shoulder. Her happy scent surrounds me as I close my eyes begging for help from anyone. At this point, if Satan were to pop up, I would probably take him up on any offer.

She presses closer and I can feel her breath on my neck. Satan doesn't need to show up. This is my hell...and my penance.

Chapter Seven

Allison

I lie in bed trying to open my eyes. It's hard because they hurt. In fact, my entire body aches, from the top of my head to my tippy toes. I have no one to blame but myself—and Savannah. I never really partied in college, but that's probably because Savannah went to culinary school in California. The woman could entice the saintiest person to sin. Santiest isn't a word but...what was I thinking?

Oh, yeah, I hurt. Now my head is pounding not only from my misadventures from the night before, but also from thinking thoughts. Jesus. I think my eyelashes hurt. I am a mess and again, my fault. Well, I think I can also blame my friends—especially Savannah. Also, I think something crawled into my mouth and died. Good God, what did I eat last night? I could probably kill people with my breath. They could bottle up the smell and use it against any enemy.

Knowing that it isn't going to get better, I force my

lids to raise enough so I can see in my room. It's dark, but I feel it's later in the morning. The crack of thunder up above tells me we're having thunderstorms. The wind rushes through the trees and even that causes me pain. Every sound jackhammers agony in my head. What had I been thinking?

I didn't think. That's why I got into trouble. I was sad about having a staycation by myself. It would be different if I could spend time with someone and we could do fun things together. But I decided I would spend my staycation working around the house. I hadn't had a choice because the hospital only lets me have so much leave transfer from year-to-year.

I drag myself out of bed and stumble into the bathroom. I'm not nauseous, thank God, but my body hurts. How did I get so old that I can't go have fun with my friends? Every little inch of my body throbs with misery and suffering.

After I brush my teeth and relieve myself, I step back into my bedroom. I strip out of my dress and panties, then grab an oversized T-shirt. There's no reason I have to get dressed today. Besides, I might hurt too much. Today will involve resting and binging shows I'm behind on. And dammit, I have to go to the grocery store.

I hear a clink in the distance, and I know it's in my house. Instantly, my body goes on alert. I can't remember how I got home. Did I bring a guy home with me? I remember we were talking about Ed and how much I wanted him, then we chatted about Austin and why he was unsuitable...

Another clang. I glance at my bed. There is an impression on right side. Definitely an adult slept there, but not me. I can never fall asleep on the right side of my bed.

Oh, no. This is just like a Discovery ID show. They will talk about how dedicated I was to my patients, but one night, I went home with a stranger and he killed me. Or that's what they are assuming because they can't find my body.

I hear a buzzing and notice my phone on the bedside table. It's blowing up.

EJ: *If you don't answer me, I'll call the police.*

Then there are like fifty other messages on there. Good lord, Austin should have taken their phones away from them last night. Most of it is drunken gibberish about yangs and yings. What the hell?

Savannah: *You are texting too loud again. I want to die.*

Me: *I know the feeling.*

EJ: *At least we know you're alive. What happened last night?*

Me: *Did I leave with anyone?*

EJ: *I can't remember. It's really hazy.*

Savannah: *I'm dead. I can't help you.*

I could tell them I'm in the house with a stranger, but then they would yell at me via text. Worse, they might just call the police. Especially EJ. She grew up in Savannah and while it's not a small town, it still has that feel. She's the first to freak out and assume the worst.

I draw in a deep breath and slink down the hallway,

baseball bat in hand. The kitchen light is on and whoever is in there is not trying to be quiet. Then I hear a mumbled curse and I recognize the voice.

Ed Cooper is in my house? I step around the corner and watch as he takes something out of the oven. Ed Cooper is in my house *and* baking?

He almost drops the pan of muffins when he turns around.

"Jesus, Allison, what the hell are you doing?"

I shrug fighting the need to cry. The throbbing in my body now has a sexual component to it. "I could ask you the same thing."

"I'm baking."

"That's apparent. But why are you doing it in my house?" And why do you look so right in my kitchen? I'm never going to be able to be there now without picturing Ed standing there looking grumpy. Life isn't fair.

"What are you wearing?" he asks in a strangled voice.

I look down and remember I threw on a T-shirt that hits me at mid-thigh. It's not like I'm standing there in lingerie. Mainly because I don't have much—and that's kind of embarrassing to admit even to myself.

"A t-shirt."

"You need to put on some pants, Allison," he says, as he stares at my legs. Wait, why is he staring at my legs? I don't think I have ever seen that expression before. Slowly, his gaze travels up my body. The pain of my hangover dissolves as a rush of hormones flies through me. My nipples are hard—something that's probably easy for him to see—and my pussy is pulsing—something I hope he cannot tell. By the time he makes eye contact, my entire body feels as if he's lit a match to it. I resist the urge to fidget. Barely.

"Allison."

Just my name, but it's the sexiest my name has ever sounded before.

"What?"

"You. Need. More. Clothes."

He utters every word as if he is barely holding onto his control. "My house, my rules. Besides, you can't see anything."

His eyes narrow and there's a tick in his cheek. "Your brother would not agree."

"I bet you think I should put panties on too."

Another mutter that sounds something like 'fuck me' under his breath.

"I don't understand what's wrong. My bathing suit shows more skin."

He slams the muffin tin down on the counter and raises his gaze to mine.

"I'll tell you what's bothering me," he says, his voice shimmering with barely controlled anger and something else...something that sounds a lot like arousal. "You plastered yourself all over me last night and then called me hard."

"I did what?" I screech.

He shoves his hand through his hair and leaves it sexy and disheveled. How do guys do that? "Every day I have to deal with you in my shop."

"I think my brother and Fritz would say it was their shop too."

He ignores that comment. He's a man on a mission, whatever that might be. His gaze is direct, dark, and so, so sexy. Warmth takes up residence between my legs, sending a gush of liquid to my pussy. Oh, my. Sexy, smiling Ed Cooper is a thing to behold. This Ed Cooper... well, let's just say if I did have a pair of panties on, they would be drenched.

"Then you tell me you want me inside of you."

The second he tells me that, pieces of the previous night start coming together, and I feel my face flush in embarrassment. I *did* tell him that. Jesus, I need to never drink again. Ever. Especially not tequila. That shit is going to be the death of me because I *am* going to die of humiliation.

He's still staring at me like I'm evil incarnate. I decide to pretend like I didn't just remember everything I did the night before.

"That sounds like a lie."

"Excuse me?" he says from behind clenched teeth. Ed looks a little angry right now, and maybe I should just get him out of my house. Mainly because I want to hide under the covers and pretend that last night never happened. I am *never* drinking tequila again. *Ever*.

"I appreciate that you brought me home, but you didn't need to stay. And you definitely don't need to make me muffins."

"I had to because you had nothing to eat. Jesus, you should have more than a bottle of crappy chardonnay and moldy cheese, Allison. You're a nurse. You know to eat better."

"I was going to HEB today."

"I did it for you."

I blink. "Wait, what? You went shopping for me?"

His expression changes a little and his face flushes. "I thought you needed something other than coffee for breakfast."

"And you made me coffee?"

He hesitates. "I needed some, so I made a pot."

"Oh," is all I can say. It was sweet in a way that he went shopping for me, but I hate that he's making me feel like an idiot. I work ten-hour days and sometimes I just pick up something to eat on the way home. Also, this is my staycation, so I had planned on shopping this morning.

"Allison," he says, again from behind clenched teeth.

I frown because I don't like that tone and he's using it a lot this morning. I mean, he's in my kitchen being kind of a butthead, so why is he so irritated with me? Is he mad at me for coming onto him? That could be it. There's a good chance I was kind of handsy last night. I tend to do that when I drink. Being mad about something like that is just silly. I mean, embarrassed, I can understand that.

"What?" I ask when I realize he's waiting for an answer.

"For the love of the baby Jesus, get some clothes on."

I blink and look down again, then back up at him. There's a flush to his skin that has nothing to do with embarrassment. His hands are on the counter and clenched into fists as if he's trying to control himself. Then, I raise my gaze to his once again.

"Why?"

He growls...GROWLS...at me. The man is sexy no matter what he's doing, but he's especially sexy when he's standing in my kitchen after baking me muffins and growling at me. He would be sexy if he just stood there and breathed.

"Just..." he closes his eyes and takes a deep breath. "Just go get dressed. Please."

The last word comes out as a half plea-half growl. I told him he was hard...asked him to be inside of me...and he looks like he's ready to tackle me. Not at all Ed-like.

"Maybe I don't want to."

His eyes narrow. "What?"

"I heard you, but see, Ed, I don't take orders in my house."

"Is that a fact?" he asks, every word seemingly pulled from somewhere deep inside of him. I'm not stupid, but I might be ignorant of what Ed's moods are like. No, strike that. I know all of them, but this is a new one for me. He's irritated and ordering me to put clothes on. Is he attracted to me? Is that why he's acting like a bear?

Those thoughts give me courage to walk towards him, placing the bat against the side of the island. His only movement is his chest. He's gulping in deep breaths. And his eyes. He follows my every move. A tiny little thrill dances down my spine. If I had panties on, they would be soaked. I know because I can feel my inner lips dampen with every step I take towards Ed.

"Yeah. I'm in charge of my house and if I want to stand here just wearing my shirt, I can do that." I stop next to him and raise up to my tiptoes. God, there is that sugary scent I love so much...and warm, delicious man. The mix of scents are so intoxicating. "Especially without panties," I say, almost a whisper, but it might as well have been an explosion.

He turns his head to look at me, his hands still fisted on the counter. When he makes eye contact, my heart rate kicks up a notch. Heat flares in his eyes.

"You're playing with fire, Allison." His voice sounds like gravel, a deep rumble that I can feel all the way to the soles of my feet. Just hearing him say my name adds to the hunger growing inside me.

I lean closer, letting my breast brush against his arm as I sink back down off my toes. He shudders at the touch. His gaze drops down to my mouth. I lick my lips, pulling another growl from him. Arousal threads through me and I press my thighs together as my clit throbs with need. I'm wet, embarrassingly so. I add everything up in my head. The stories from my friends about him looking at me, along with the way he's acting, makes me think there is more to it than just being a good friend. It gives me enough courage to raise up again, then lean closer again, pressing my aching breasts against him. I almost moan at the contact. There is no doubt he can feel how hard my nipples are.

"I'd rather play with you, Ed."

Chapter Eight

For a long few seconds, I stand there, unable to do anything other than stare at her. She's the object of all my desires, the woman who stars in every one of my most erotic dreams. And she just said she wanted to play with me. There's precum in my pants again. Jesus. She's rubbing against me like a cat, and all I want to do is make her pretty pussy purr for me.

"I'm not sure that's a good idea," I say, barely able to speak.

She leans closer, hunger darkening her eyes. I can feel her nipples poking into my arm. Still, I can't move. That would require a functioning brain. I waved goodbye to that particular organ sometime after she said she wasn't wearing panties.

"I have to disagree, Ed." She brushes her mouth against mine, then says, "I think it's the best idea I've had in a while."

Jesus fuck. I want to take her down on the floor and

fuck her like some kind of goddamn animal. That's how far gone I am. I can smell her, that sunshiny scent I love. She shivers and I lose it. There is no way I can resist her, not when she is almost naked and begging me to play with her. With a groan, I grab her as I turn my entire body toward her.

"I warned you," I breathe out, giving her that one last chance to run away.

"I'm calling your bluff," she says, pressing against me and moaning when she comes in contact with my cock. A shudder of need courses through me, leaving me almost breathless.

I look down just as she raises her chin. I've seen that look before, and I know she's definitely going to hold me to my challenge. With a groan, I swoop down for a quick, hard kiss before lifting her up onto the kitchen island. Stepping between her legs, I jerk her to the edge, pushing her shirt up. With each inch of flesh revealed, I feel my control slipping from my grasp. I've wanted her for over a year, ignoring the beat of lust that pounded through my body every time she was near. Now that I've gotten my hands on her, I don't have to ignore it. I can give into it like the heathen that I am.

I lean in and kiss her, keeping my eyes open until hers slide closed. I deepen the kiss, sliding my tongue along the seam of her lips. They part easily and I steal in for a taste. Cupping her face with both hands, I slant my mouth over hers again and again. Her skin is soft, almost like a rose petal.

She returns my kiss with a hum and sucking on my

tongue. Mother fucking sucking my tongue. Jesus. The hum vibrates from my tongue all the way through every inch of my body. I shudder as I slide my hands down her body, brushing the sides of her breasts. When I reach her thighs, I tear my mouth away and press her legs further apart and drop down to my knees.

She didn't lie about not wearing panties. Her dark hair is trimmed and allows an amazing view of her cunt. Pink and glistening and ready for me. Still, I need a taste. Leaning closer, I draw in her scent. God fucking damn, even her pussy smells like sunshine.

"Sunshine?" she asks, and I realize I said something out loud.

I look up at her and she is smiling down at me. "You always smell of sunshine and happiness."

Her face flushes. "I do not."

"You do."

I don't wait for a response. Instead, I kiss one thigh, then the other, keeping my mouth pressed against her flesh as I trail kisses up to her mound. I lean closer, drawing in more of her earthy scent mixed with her usual warm scent. Nothing in this world could smell as good as Allison's cute little kitty. I'm sure of it. My mouth waters thinking about just how good it is going to taste. I've been wanting this for what seems like forever, and there is a small part of me that just wants to devour her.

I slip my tongue inside, and groan when the flavor of her arousal hits my taste buds. I feel my control slipping, as I move up to her clit. I slide a finger between her wet folds as I drag my teeth against the tiny bundle of nerves.

She shifts her legs wider and presses against my face. I am lost in her, her scent, her taste. The thought of how tight her cunt will wrap around my dick has me almost coming. I jerk at the button on my jeans and then slide the zipper down. My cock springs free. I wrap my hand around it, squeezing it at the base to try to hold off my own orgasm as I continue to tease Allison.

Her moans are growing in volume as I add another finger. She's so fucking wet my fingers are dripping with her dewy arousal. I know my beard is wet with it. I don't give a fuck. She's beyond delicious, the sweetest treat I've ever had the pleasure to savor. I suck her clit into my mouth and curl my digits inside of her. Another round of shivers rolls through her, but she is still not there, not to the pinnacle. She jerks against my mouth and her cunt clamps down hard on my fingers as she screams out my name.

As I look up at her, I continue to thrust in and out of her, helping her ride the wave of her orgasm. Watching her shudder is one of the most erotically beautiful things I have seen. She is still shivering when I finally pull my fingers from her. She's smiling, her face flushed, but her entire body relaxed from her orgasm. I rub my fingers against her mouth.

"Open up, Sunshine," I say, and she complies as her eyes open. I slip my fingers into her mouth. "See, you *do* taste like sunshine."

She sucks on my digits, sliding her tongue around them, and I almost pass out. I jerk my fingers from her mouth, then grab her by the hips and hoist her on my shoulder. I start off to her bedroom, because if I don't get there in the next few seconds, I might just fuck her on the kitchen counter. Which isn't a bad idea, but the first time I have her, I want it to be in that bed of hers.

She reaches down, slipping her hands beneath my jeans and grabs my ass. I almost drop her.

"Woman," I say, swatting her rear end.

"What? I've been having fantasies about your butt for years."

I pause in the hallway. "Years?"

"Yep. I can't wait to see it up close and personal." The way her voice deepens and the fact that she's still sliding her hands over my ass pushes me closer to the edge..

"Jesus," I say once again.

She's going to be the death of me. I step into her bedroom and toss her on the bed. She laughs, the sound of it so joyous I'm momentarily transfixed. She's always been a happy person, someone who always had a smile for me. For everyone. I know it's why she is such a good nurse. Happiness and sunshine. Every time I'm near her, I feel it shower over me. Now, I get to feel it as I slip inside of her.

Her laughter fades the longer I stand there staring at her. "What?"

I shake my head not wanting to say anything to scare her away. If Allison knew the depth of my feelings, she would probably run from me. She should. But she lost that right when she challenged me. Now, she's mine.

"If you like that shirt, you might want to take it off," I

say as I tug my shirt over my head and slide my jeans down and step out of them. "Otherwise, I'm gonna tear it off you."

As she tosses her shirt, I stand transfixed again. She's a fucking goddess. Her skin is almost flawless, except for the few freckles on her shoulders, which I find sexy. I know at that moment, I have probably lost my mind because who the fuck finds freckles sexy? I do as long as they inhabit Allison's flesh. My gaze drops lower. Her breasts are tipped with the rosiest nipples. As I continue on the path down her body, I realize she was perfectly made for me. She's curvy in all the right spots, all hills and valleys, and I know that her flesh tastes sweeter than any buttercream frosting. My hands are shaking my need is so fierce, so I settle them on my hips.

"I see I'm not the only one without any underwear."

"Complaining?"

She shakes her head, pulling her bottom lip between her teeth. It's something she does when she's trying to control her smile. It's cute, but I would much rather have her smile. Before I can say anything, she reaches over to her side table and grabs a box of condoms.

"Been busy?" I ask, letting my brows rise up as I stamp down on my jealousy. It's stupid to be jealous of men before me, but I can't help it. More than likely, they were better for her than I ever will be.

"Not really. I threw the other box out because it reached the expiration date."

Now it's my turn to smile. She pulls out a condom

and tosses it at me. I catch it easily, ripping it open and rolling it down my cock.

I look up and see that's she's watching my hands. "What?"

"That's one of the sexiest things I've seen a man do."

Her voice deepens over the words, and it's easy to hear the arousal. Still. Even after she came all over my mouth.

I crawl onto the bed and cover her body with mine. I flex my hips, pressing my cock against her pussy. Even through the condom, I can feel how wet she is. I drag the head down her slit and she shudders. That little reaction is everything. It is damning me to hell, but she's like a drug and I am the addict who can't resist.

I raise up enough to position my cock at her entrance. I know she's wet enough, so I thrust in hard, fierce, all the way to the hilt. She gasps, then moans as her cunt pulses around my dick. I have to grit my teeth to keep from coming. I want her with me when I finally give in. I raise up to my knees, dragging her up to meet my thrusts. At first, I can keep the rhythm measured, easily drawing her closer to another orgasm. But soon, the feel of her pussy squeezing my dick, the way her moans are filling the air around us, and the sight of her laid out before me, has my control slipping from my grasp. Her breasts jiggle every time I drive back into her. She wraps her legs around my waist, then raises her hands up to hold on to her headboard. Harder and harder, I thrust into her. Bending my head, I take one nipple into my mouth. That's enough to push her up to the peak. She bucks against me as her orgasm tears through her. Her pussy clamps down tight, pulling my own release from me. I groan out her name as I thrust into her one more time. I collapse on top of her.

I lay there, waiting for the guilt, waiting for something to tell me I shouldn't have done that, but nothing comes. All I feel is...happy. I'm so fucking happy and content that I almost laugh, but I don't. I only smile. And if this is what making love to Allison feels like, I could do this every day for the rest of my life.

Chapter Nine

Allison

We lay in the silence of my room, our breathing the only sound filling the air around us. Our skin is sticky with exertion and right now I don't give a flying flip. I smile as I slip a finger down his spine. He shivers.

He attempts to move away from me, but I tighten my arms and legs around him. He's still inside of me and I like that feeling. I squeeze him tight with my inner muscles. So decadent. Nothing will ever compare to having Ed deep inside of me. "Nope, not letting you go, Edward."

He chuckles and I can feel it everywhere. Against my chest, my stomach, and even inside of me.

"Not going anywhere, Sunshine."

I smile at the nickname. The idea that he thought that about me makes me so freaking giddy. All of the sudden, we're rolling over the bed and I'm sitting on top of him. He's still inside of me and I look down at him.

"As long as you understand that." I smile at him and settle my hands against his chest.

He returns my smile and I can't help but sigh. A little happy sigh. The man is definitely gorgeous, but here in my bed, with the sun dancing over his flesh...he's amazing.

"What are you thinking, Edward Cooper?"

"I was thinking of what next I could do to your body."

I feel my face heat. "Yeah? Like what?"

"Lots of things," he says as he slips a finger over my nipple before giving it a tug. *Oh, my*. Just that one little touch has me craving for more.

"How about you show me that amazing shower?" he asks.

He really didn't answer my question, but right now, the idea of having Ed in my shower is enough to make me happy.

"That sounds fantastic." I lean down and brush my mouth against his. Part of me wants to take a shower with Ed, and part of me wants to stay right here. Having him in my bed has been my ultimate fantasy. If I leave this bed, he might disappear on me.

"What's that look?" he asks.

I shake my head, but he reaches up and brushes his fingers over my jaw. The touch of his callused hands sends a wave of longing that almost chokes me. This right here. This is all I need in the world.

"Tell me."

I sigh. "I'm worried that things will go back to the way it was before."

His eyes widen and then his lips curve...slowly... sexily...holy crap the man is sexy as all fuck.

"I said before, I'm not giving you up. You're mine and I'll beat the crap out of anyone who says you're not."

Something loosens in my chest and I find my own lips start to curve. "Yeah?'

"Try me, Sunshine."

I giggle and lean down to brush my mouth over his. "Always."

He growls and I giggle again. "I like that sound," he says.

I say nothing to that because I'm feeling kind of weepy at the moment. Instead, I pull away and then lift myself off his cock. We both groan. He's still hard, but I slip out of bed, and head to the bathroom. He follows and steps in, removing his condom and throwing it in the trash. I start the shower to let the water warm up. There were three things that sold the house to me when I first saw it. The backyard, which I'm still working on, but has a lot of mature trees and shade. Second is the kitchen. I might not be a master baker, but I do like to cook. It looks like it could be featured in the after pictures on Fixer Upper. Marble countertops, a six-burner stove, a farmhouse sink, and lots of open shelving. And then there is the master bath. My house was originally built in the 60's, so I know that this was a complete remodel. There's a clawfoot tub in one corner and a seamless shower next to it.

"I guess we could have taken a bath," he says stepping behind me. His cock presses against my rear and I have to shiver once again. How is it that this man can reduce me to a puddle of hormones without even trying? Because he is Ed-freaking-Cooper. That's the only explanation I need.

I glance at the bathtub. "I guess we could."

"Naw, we'll spend too much time in it. And I'm hungry for more than mind blowing sex."

He says it easily enough that I glance over my shoulder.

"What?" he asks, letting one of his eyebrows rise. I shrug.

"So, this isn't just a one-day thing?"

He grunts—a very sexy sound—and eyes me as if I've lost my mind. "Not fucking likely, Sunshine."

I grin. "Good."

"I told you that you were mine. I'm not fucking around."

I chuckle. "Well, a little bit of fucking around."

Steam is billowing out of the shower and I know that the water is no longer frigid. I step in and he follows me. I've never taken a shower with a man before. Hell, it's been so long since I've had a man in my bed, and I've never had a man here in my house overnight.

"Hand me the soap," Ed says. He's shielding me from the spray with his massive body, but when I hand him my herbal soap, he steps back so my back gets wet. Before I know it, he steps closer and presses his soapy hands to my back.

"Oh, God, that feels good."

He chuckles and works my muscles beneath the suds. Magic hands.

"I was thinking."

"Sometimes a dangerous thing," I say.

He chuckles. "I'd like to take you out on my bike."

"Hmm, that sounds like fun."

"Yeah?" he asks, surprise in his voice.

I glance over my shoulder at him. "You know I've asked before."

"You were seventeen and your father was shaking his head behind you."

"That jerk. I am going to give him a piece of my mind."

"Ah, Sunshine, don't rat me out."

I chuckle. My father might have been a hard ass when he was younger, but he was probably no Ed Cooper. Ed's big, tall, muscled and a total badass. But the fear I hear in his voice makes me think he's afraid of my father.

"Have you always thought of me like that? Like Sunshine?"

"No. Well, at first, yeah. Harry brought me home and you were such a cute little thing. So in a completely non sexual way at first."

"And then?"

He grunts. "Then, very sexual."

"When?"

"When?"

I roll my eyes. "Yeah, when did you start having sexual thoughts about me?"

"When we got back to San Antonio."

"Two years," I exclaim and then turn to face him. I smack him in the chest. "Two years!"

"Almost. Yeah, so?"

"We could have been having incredible sex all this time."

He chuckles. "That's true. I didn't think you thought of me that way."

"Of course I did. I do! Who doesn't? I bet every heterosexual woman does."

His face flushes.

"Oh, my, you're blushing."

"Am not."

I giggle. "Yeah you are and it's damned cute. You've always thought of me as Sunshine then?"

"In my head."

"Yeah?'

"Why are you so surprised?"

I shrug and reach for the soap he's still holding. He raises his hand so high I can't grab it. "Ed."

"Allison," he says. "Don't tell me you think you aren't sexy."

"I know I'm a nurse who takes care of everyone."

He shakes his head. "Like in a hot nurse costume kind of a way."

I roll my eyes. "Please don't even mention that. Nurses hate it, including me."

His mouth twitches. "Stop trying to change the subject. You're sexy."

I pat him on the chest. "Okay."

"I will paddle that very sexy ass of yours. Don't try to fucking placate me."

"Is that a promise?" I ask.

He leans his head back as he pinches his eyes shut. "For the love of the baby Jesus."

I giggle again and fall against him. He slips one arm around me, then puts down the soap so he can wrap me completely in both arms. My breasts are pressed against him, namely my diamond hard nipples. And hello, his cock is against my pussy.

"You're sexy, Allison. I don't know what kind of assholes you've been dating, other than that Kent guy, who I know for sure was an asshole."

"How do you know that?" He was, but I never said anything in front of Ed about it.

"He gave you up, didn't he?" He cups my face. Water is beating down on him, his hair is plastered against his head and he shouldn't look sexy, but he does. "Every part of your body is sexy."

"Yeah?'

He nods as he leans closer to brush his mouth against mine, then he kisses my nose.

"Your nose is sexy." I snort laugh, and he doesn't say anything, but he does smile. He lets go of my face to turn me around.

"Brace your hands against the wall."

I do as he says because he's touching me. There is a very good chance if Ed asked me to kill someone, I would as long as he was touching me. Okay, maybe not kill someone, but you get what I mean.

He trails his hand down my spine, his fingers dancing over my slick skin. "Now, this part of you," he says as his index finger slides down the cleft of my rear end before he spreads his hands over my cheeks. "This is one of my favorite parts of you."

God, I can barely think, breathe...anything. The man is undoing me, not just with his hands, but also his words. Not one man has ever said the things he's saying about me today. Even Kent, who lasted a whole year. He rarely even worried if I came.

The first smack to my ass catches me off guard. The sting makes me gasp as the warmth of it spreads. Then another smack. This one I feel all the way to my core.

"Don't think bad thoughts," he orders.

"How can you know I was thinking anything bad?"

"First, you just confirmed it. Second, you weren't with me."

He's right because I was thinking about Kent the not so wonderful lover.

Ed lays his hand against my ass again and I realize he really is going to spank me if I keep this up. But then, as the shivers of the last smack roll through me, I think that might not be such a bad thing. Maybe, I should be bad Allison. The one who likes to be spanked in her shower.

Unfortunately, Ed has other ideas.

"Now, here," he says as he slips his hands around to my stomach. He skims them up to my breasts, "Are two of my favorites."

He plucks at my nipples and I moan, leaning back against him and pressing my rear end against his cock. Heat is pouring through my entire body. I'm beyond wet, as another gush of liquid fills my pussy. My clit is throbbing, begging to be touched, but he is taking his time teasing my breasts. Every time one of those talented fingers glide over my nipple, I can feel it in my sex. He plucks at one of them and I swear to all that is holy that my clit stands up and shouts for attention.

As he crowds against me, he leans down and presses his mouth over my exposed neck. He continues to murmur something, but I can't make it out. I don't care. Right now, all I care about is how he is playing my body like I'm an instrument.

He continues to drive me insane by nipping at my neck and teasing my nipple, then he slides his right hand down past my stomach, resting it against my mound. My clit hums. Seriously. I'm not lying. It's like she's waiting, anticipating what Ed is going to do to her. What? I call my clit a she. Get over it.

He kisses a path up to my ear and tugs on the lobe. "Now, this little kitty here," he says as he brushes his fingers over my slit, barely touching my clit, who is waving at him because she's been ready to come out and play from the moment he spanked me, "this might be my favorite part by far." He slips one digit inside of me and I buck against him. Just that little touch has me spiraling. Good lord.

"Yeah, I have to say she's my favorite," he says, his

voice all gravely and sexy and all Ed. "So tight, always wet for me. You're wet for me, aren't you, Sunshine?"

I nod, unable to say anything. My ability to speak is directly linked to his fingers. As I think that, Ed slips another digit inside of me. "God."

"No, Sunshine, just you and me."

I would laugh if my whole body wasn't vibrating with need. Right now, I want to come, but I also don't want it to end. I know I sound like an idiot, but I don't care. I don't care about anything but Ed's fingers, and his mouth. Yeah, I like his mouth. And his dick. He moves his mouth down my neck again and nips against my shoulder. I'm close, but he's avoiding my clit. I know he's doing it on purpose because there are two things I know about Ed Cooper. First, he's the best baker in all of Texas. Secondly, he knows just how to make a woman come. So, he's definitely doing it on purpose and that is kind of annoying. I open my mouth to complain but end up squeaking—yeah, I'm a sexy beast—when he pulls away and turns me around.

He cups my face and lowers his mouth to mine. In that kiss I taste his need. It sends my heart galloping out of control. I don't know exactly what the hell I'm going to do about him, if this really is the start to a serious relationship. At the moment, nothing matters but this kiss. I'm drowning, falling under his spell. I wrap my arms around him and return the kiss. He hums—God, he hums—against my tongue as I slide it into his mouth. Before I'm ready, he pulls away to rest his forehead against mine.

"You are dangerous." His breathing is ragged, and his

voice is still all growly, and all I want to do is jump on him and take a ride on the Ed Cooper pony patrol. Or stallion. I press against his cock. Yep, definitely a stallion. He urges me back against the wall. "Especially this little kitty," he says as he slips down to his knees in front of me. "She's the most dangerous part of you."

He leans closer, pushing his face between my legs. His beard tickles my thighs and I sigh. Ed's the first bearded man I've had, and I'm not sure I will ever date another clean-shaved man again. It adds another level to oral sex. He slips his tongue inside, teasing my inner lips. I buck against him and he growls—yes growls, again. I never thought I would be a woman who liked that kind of sound, but with it coming from Ed, I can't resist him. It gets sexier every time he does it. Taking hold of my hips, he anchors me to the tile all the while he is devouring me. It's the only word I can think of. He's still growling against my flesh, sending another round of vibrations rolling through me. I don't think a man has ever tasted me like this, as if I was the only thing in the world that could save him. As he continues to explore my pussy, he slips one hand to my clit. Over and over, he thrusts his tongue inside of me as he grazes my clit with his thumb. God. That one little touch has me so damned close I'm ready to come right there. One more feathery touch, then he presses his thumb against the bundle of nerves, sending me hurtling over into my orgasm. Pleasure shimmers through me and explodes, over and over, as I buck against his mouth. I slip my hands through his hair, then mold them to the back of his head as he eats me through my orgasm. It is the most decadent thing I have ever had done to me, and I don't think I will be able to forget it. Not even if the men in black show up with one of their little memory zappers.

I can barely stand by the time the little aftershocks are the only thing pulsing through me, but thankfully, Ed holds on to me as he rises to his feet.

"Are you on the pill?"

I nod.

"Been tested?"

I raise one eyebrow, but he gets the drift. It's the only thing I can do because I am still trying to recover from the orgasm he just gave me.

"I have too, and I'm clean."

I know what he's asking. Normally, I wouldn't trust a man, but this is Ed and I know he's not lying. I nod, giving him approval. He sighs, lifting me up against the tile and thrusts into me to the hilt. I draw in a deep breath because while I am wet, I am still sensitive from my orgasm.

"Oh, fuck, Sunshine," he says, the timber of his voice rumbling over my nickname. "I have never been raw inside a woman before."

His cock pulses inside of me for a long second, then he starts to move. He pounds into me over and over. His breathing is labored and he's watching me. The intensity of his gaze scares me a little. There is a piece of him that I never thought I would see. That raw need. Emotions rise up and claw at my throat. This is beyond intimate, it's something I have never felt before. I want to look away, but I know what he wants, what he needs. I need that too, but needing it scares the hell out of me. But I'm sick of being scared of always worrying about if I should be careful. Right now, with this man, I don't want to be careful. I want it all.

I wrap my legs around him and squeeze. His eyes practically roll back in his head. He changes the angle of his thrusts so he's rubbing against my clit and his cock is hitting right there...oh God...my g-spot. I come apart again, splintering into a million different pieces. He thrusts one more time, then holds himself still as his warm cum fills my pussy. He continues to hold himself still there for a few moments, his cock pulsing inside of me as we both shudder from our orgasms. He has his head against my shoulder and his hands and body are still holding me in place.

He pulls back, then brushes his mouth against my forehead first then my nose, then, he kisses me. I can feel everything in that one kiss, everything I was afraid to want for the longest time, but it's there, shimmering in the kiss he gives me. When he pulls back, we are both breathing heavily, and I realize that the water is cooling off.

"You definitely deserve breakfast after that."

I smile, happiness in my heart and my soul. "I think you are the one who should get breakfast served."

He shakes his head, his smile fading as his expression turns serious. "No, Sunshine, letting me bake for you is one of my favorite things to do."

My heart turns over. "If it makes you happy, you can bake for me as much as you like."

I barely bite back the words I want to say. You know, the, *you can bake for me for the rest of our lives* kind of words. No reason to scare off Ed. Right now, I am going to try my best to live in the moment and enjoy Ed.

Chapter Ten

Ed

"So," Allison says, sipping her coffee and giving the sexiest little hum, "You've called me Sunshine in your head for two years?"

I nod as I dip the bread in the egg mixture. She requested French toast, so she gets French toast. If she requested her brother's head on a platter, I would do it in a heartbeat. Not that I don't love Harry like a brother, but Allison gets what she wants. Period.

"Actually, like I said, it was before that."

"Hmm." She takes another sip of her coffee. "God that's good. I make crappy coffee."

"Yeah you do. And what's wrong with the name Sunshine?"

I make sure the griddle is well-greased and drop the bread on it. The smell of vanilla, cinnamon, and nutmeg fill the kitchen as the egg mixture sizzles on the stove. It feeds my soul on another level I can't always explain to other people. I went without food so many days growing up, but the idea of cooking for others, creating something they love to eat, makes me feel whole. Doing it here in the kitchen with Allison, with the sun trying to peek through the clouds, is like heaven.

"Well, I just think it sounds cute."

"You are cute and sexy," I say.

I get to play with our kitchen at work, but this set up is amazing. Allison likes to cook, I know that, but she doesn't do much baking. Not her thing. But this kitchen is definitely a chef's dream. I remember Savannah commenting on it when Allison moved in. The six-burner Viking, the marble countertops, and the farm-house sink. It's amazing.

I glance back over my shoulder at Allison. She's still frowning. "Alright, you can give me a nickname."

"I already have one for you."

Then she presses her lips together as if she regretted telling me. I turn back to the French toast and flip them over. Then I turn my attention to her again.

"You have a name for me?"

Her face flushes, and she hides behind the massive cup as she sips her coffee. Interesting.

"No fair. Spill."

She mumbles something I can't quite hear. That's not normal because Allison is not a woman who mumbles. She's usually as loud as those other two insane friends of hers, but now she's acting like she's afraid to talk.

"What was that?" I ask, holding my hand up to my ear.

She glances at me one more time, then frowns.

"I will not give you any French toast unless you tell me my nickname."

Her dramatic gasp is so Allison. You can do a lot of things to Allison, but threatening her food is a crime.

I turn back to the food and flip the toast over. "Worse, I will pile it high on one plate and eat it in front of you."

Which I wouldn't, but she doesn't know that. I just know what can get her to talk.

She says nothing as I plate the French toast, doing as I said I would, stacking it high on one plate. I set it on the counter and prepare it. After slathering on a fuck-ton of butter, I drown it in syrup and then—the thing I know that will break her—I dust it with powdered sugar. I'm cutting into the bread when she sighs loudly.

"Fine."

She hesitates and I dig into the piece I cut off and raise it to my lips.

"Ed."

"Tell me, or I eat it all."

She sighs and looks at the fork, then back at me. "I call you Ginger Jesus."

I blink. That can't be what I thought she said. "Ginger Jesus?"

"Yeah."

"What? When?"

"How? Who?"

"Allison." I use the tone of voice that used to make grown men piss their pants, but she rolls her eyes. Damn, I love her. "Explain."

"Ginger Jesus. I started calling you that in my head when you all opened Camos and Cupcakes. You know, like they call Ed Sheehan because you're both gingers." Her gaze roams over me before she makes eye contact again. My body vibrates with hunger. With one look. That's all she apparently needs to do to bring me to my knees. "Although, you're ten times sexier than he is. Plus, you make the most amazing cupcakes. And cakes. And oh, I love your chocolate chip peanut butter cookies."

"I know."

"You know I call you Ginger Jesus? Who told you? Savannah? No, she wouldn't tell you. EJ. It was EJ. That woman is in so much trouble. Or was it my mother?"

"Your mother?" Jesus holy fuck balls, Mrs. B knows. "No. I mean, I know you like my chocolate chip peanut butter cookies."

"Yeah?"

I nod. "Yeah. You make the most amazing little mewling sounds when you're eating something you like."

"Oh," she says. "That's kind of embarrassing."

"Not as embarrassing as walking around with a boner because I was watching you eat a cupcake."

She laughs as I divide the food between two plates. "You do not."

I set one plate in front of her, then climb on the stool next to hers. "Yeah. Yesterday was a close thing. Your brother walked in while you were eating your cupcake and it was embarrassing. There I was thinking about getting you naked and your brother's talking to me. It was weird."

She smiles. "Yeah, I know what you mean. Sometimes I would watch you frosting a cupcake and I'd get aroused."

"Yeah, like how?"

"Let's just say that it wasn't that cold out, but you couldn't tell that by looking at my nipples. Also, I had to change my panties."

It surprises a laugh out of me. Allison isn't a prude, that's for sure.

She cuts into her French toast with her fork. She slips it between her plump lips and hums...HUMS...and then sighs. Fuck, that is the sexiest thing I've seen. Well, it ranks up there in the top five moments where Allison almost made me come in my pants. She notices me watching her eat. "What?"

My body is primed, ready to drag her back into the bedroom and show her just what that moan does to me. Jesus, the woman is going to kill me.

"Just, eat."

Her eyes widen and then a slow smile curves her full lips. She says nothing but digs back into her food. And there, with the quietness of the Sunday morning, we eat and talk like I don't want to do so many horrible things that involve her and frosting.

WE CLEAN the kitchen up together. I never thought I would find something as easy as rinsing dishes and washing griddles romantic, but then, I never had Allison before. She laughs over a story about one of their pet therapy dogs and she's snorting and...this is heaven. Surely. I never had a regular life before I entered the military. Morning routines shouldn't be so damned sweet, but the late morning light is pouring into the kitchen and her eyes are sparkling up at me and I can't stop myself.

I pull my hands out of the soapy water and cup her face. I ignore the fact that suds are slipping down my hands and onto the shirt she's wearing. She does too.

"Do you know how special you are?"

She shakes her head. "Ed..."

"You are. I've never known another person who is so happy. You make every room you walk into shine like it's the middle of a June day—even if it's midnight."

"You're making me blush, Ed."

I shake my head because I realize that she still doesn't understand what she means to me. "You know that Harry says you're the reason he held it together when your mother had breast cancer?"

She shakes her head and I see tears start to fill her eyes. Usually, I run away from a crying woman. Cowardly I know, but they make me feel completely useless. Now, though, I know that she's more important that anyone else in my life has been.

"He has always said that. And we would have never opened the store without your help. Your suggestions and your connections...you really give everything to the people you care about. It makes you special."

She opens her mouth, but she never gets to speak. Instead, another voice cuts into our idyllic morning.

"What the fuck is going on here?"

We both turn and find Harry standing in the door-way. Fuck.

Chapter Eleven

Allison

I hate my brother. Loathe him. In fact, I'm contemplating a discussion with my parents to get them to disown him. I think they would do it if I told them they could have Ed instead. He's better looking, and he can bake. Also, Ed might give them a chance at grandchildren. Not that I'm rushing into anything or expecting a proposal. Just that I would love to have a bunch of redheaded boys running around my house. If Harry loses out to Ed, we would be much better off without him around.

Said idiot brother—yeah, I called him an idiot, because he is—is wearing the same clothes he wore last night. Which means, he didn't go home. Which means, he slept with someone's sister and/or daughter. He has some nerve showing up here and judging Ed and me. See, like I said, idiot.

Harry's striding toward Ed and me like he's going to be able to take Ed down. They are about the same size, but I know Ed's tougher. Ed steps forward and shoves me behind him as if Harry would hurt me. It's kind of sweet that he thinks he needs to protect me from my brother. Interrupting my Sunday fun time with Ed—Harry will be lucky if he's able to have babies when I'm done with him.

"You want to tell me what's going on here, Cooper?"

"I think you need to watch your tone," Ed says, which makes me laugh because his tone is pretty damned mean at that moment.

"Allison, I think you need to go get dressed," Harry says. Like he has a say in the matter. Have I mentioned that he's an idiot? Well, he is.

"Why?"

"You're indecent."

I gasp, but before I can charge my brother and tackle the butthead, Ed intervenes. "You might want to get dressed since I think I hear Fritz coming through the front door."

Damn. "Fine," I say stepping around him, but he grabs me and pulls me closer.

He leans down, his mouth so close to my ear I feel his breath brush against it. "I'll handle your brother, but I'll wait until you get back."

"I can take care of myself."

He chuckles. The sound warms my soul. "I know you can, Sunshine. If you want to beat the shit out of him, I'll hold him while you do it."

And, like that, my heart lightens. I can't fight the smile curving my lips. Is it any wonder I love this man?

Big, tough, bakes cupcakes, and he's sweet. Plus, he's okay with me taking the lead.

"Oh, hey, did Ed find her..." Fritz says as he takes in the scene. "Whoa." But unlike my dumbass brother, he smiles. Then, when I step around the island, he claps his hands over his eyes. "My virgin eyes! Ugh, go away."

I ignore Fritz and step up to my brother. "If you're mean to Ed, I'll call Mom and tell her that you're ready to settle down and you want a sweet girl to do it with. Also, you want her help."

"That's mean," Fritz says, his hands still over his eyes.

"Bradleys are mean and we never fight fair. Remember that, idiot."

With that, I stomp out of the kitchen, then down the hallway to my bedroom. I can't believe he did that. Like Ed isn't good enough for me or something. Or that I am a virgin. Which I am not. Haven't been in almost ten years. I sigh and sink down on my bed.

It's just like Harry to show up right when Ed was about to say something. It was there in the depths of his blue gaze. It was as if he might offer me the world. Then my dumbass brother shows up and acts like the dumbass Ape that he is.

I glance at my phone and see I've missed some calls and texts. As I scroll through the messages and notices, I realize I missed a couple of calls and a bazillion texts from Harry. That's why he showed up. Like I sit here waiting for him to call. Then, another few text messages from EJ and Savannah, mostly about Savannah's impending death.

Me: *All of the shit has hit the preverbal fan.*

EJ: *What happened?*

Savannah: *Your text is still too loud. Stop.*

EJ: *I thought you were dead so shut up.*

Me: *My brother showed up.*

EJ: *So?*

It's then that I realize I had forgotten to text them about Ed. I was a little busy this morning.

Me: *I was wearing nothing but a big t-shirt, and Ed had his hands on me. Also, he was about to kiss me. Harry lost it.*

Savannah: *Did you take pictures of Harry getting his ass kicked? Actually, I would prefer video. It would make up for you and EJ interrupting my death.*

Me: *No. Because I had to get dressed. And Fritz showed up, but he doesn't seem that upset.*

EJ: *Is there any shouting?*

Me: *No.*

Savannah: *That's scarier.*

Panic surges through me. She's right. Loud noises are scary, but the quiet moments right before the fight might mean worse things are coming. I drop my phone on the bed and rush to get dressed. I yank off my t-shirt, grab another shirt that actually fits me, then I pull on a pair of shorts. My phone keeps pinging, so I grab it.

EJ: *You didn't tell us Ed spent the night.*

Savannah: *Yeah.*

Savannah: *Wait, did he show up at the restaurant last night?*

EJ: *He did. Then he...ohhhhhhhh :smiley face: :thumbs up: :winkyface: So you slept together last night?*

Me: *No. This morning.*

EJ: *I want details.*

Savannah: *Me too.*

Me: *Shut up, you're dead.*

EJ: *I'm alive and alone in my bed so I need the details.*

That doesn't make sense. I know EJ and she's probably already throwing clothes on because she doesn't like missing the drama. Or, Ed's cooking. She's probably hoping for some breakfast and, knowing Ed, he'll cook for her. I roll my eyes.

Me: *You're not. More than likely, you're getting dressed and coming over here.*

EJ: *DEVIL WOMAN. Stop using your magic mindreading.*

I roll my eyes.

Me: *Just get your ass over here because I might be administering first aid to my brother after Ed kicks his ass.*

Savannah: *Like I said, record that shit.*

I would usually smile at the comment, but I'm too worried about Ed and my brother. I know that Ed can handle his own, but I will not have Harry treating Ed as if he isn't good enough for me. Also, any fighting could ruin everything they've worked so hard to achieve with Camos and Cupcakes. I hurry down the hall hoping I can mediate between the two of them.

Chapter Twelve

Ed

I watch Allison walk out of the room, my heart going with her. I want to go back to our happy morning where it is just the two of us and not having a confrontation with her brother. Life never gives you good times without difficulty. I cross my arms over my chest and stare at Harry.

"So, what's new with you two?" Fritz asks as he grabs a mug. "Wait, who made the coffee?"

"I did," I say without taking my gaze from Harry.

"Good."

Harry wants to smile. I can see it in his gaze and the way his lips twitch. Everyone knows that Allison makes the shittiest coffee. Still, we're having a stare down like we're dumbass kids fighting on the playground. We're in our thirties for fuck's sake.

Fritz joins us, looking from one to the other. "Again, what's new with everyone?"

"Our former best friend here took advantage of my sister last night."

The fact that Harry would think that sends a shard of ice to my chest. Besides Fritz, he's the only brother I have on earth. We might not be related by blood, but they are my family. We went to hell and back. I know that I can call on them for help, just like they know I am here for them. The idea that he thinks I would sleep with a drunk Allison just...

"Ah, fuck, Harry get the stick out of your ass," Fritz says. He looks at me. "You didn't do that, did you?"

I shake my head.

"Then what the fuck are you doing here?" Harry mutters.

"I stayed the night to make sure she was okay." I leave out the part where she propositioned me and that I actually slept in her bed. "She was pretty drunk last night, and I worried she might need some help."

"See, not an asshole," Fritz says.

"Then why did you have your hands on her? Why were you kissing her?"

"Ohhh, you were kissing her? What was that about?"

"Fritz, if you don't shut the hell up, I'm going to punch you in the throat," Harry says.

"How rude," Fritz says as he hoists himself up on one of the barstools.

"So, I repeat, what the fuck were you doing touching my sister?" This time the words are barely above a whisper; because Harry's teeth are clenched so tight, I'm amazed he doesn't crack a tooth.

"I'm not sure that's any of your business." Because it isn't. Not really. Granted, Allison and Harry are close, but Harry has no right to say anything to me. Harry grinds his teeth together, so I decide another approach might work. "By the way, are those the same clothes you wore on your date?"

"Why?"

"Just asking."

His eyes narrow as he studies me. He knows what I'm getting at and he doesn't like it one bit.

"Oh, he has you there, Harry," Fritz says as he sips his coffee. "Tell me the sex was at least good."

"Fuck off," Harry says to him.

Fritz snickers and I know he's about to say something that will sidetrack the conversation, so I give him a look to shut him up. His eyes dance with amusement, but he says nothing else.

I look back at Harry, who is now staring at me as if I'm scum of the earth again. I have to fight the urge to rub my hand over my chest to ease the pain there.

"I still can't believe you're fucking around with my sister."

It takes every bit of my control not to punch the bastard. Mainly because that whole *having each other's back* happened and it was Harry saving my ass on deployment. And Allison. As mad as she is, she doesn't really want Harry hurt. Now if she asked me to hurt him, I would do it in a minute without a thought.

"Hey, you made French toast? Really? Why didn't you save any for me?" Fritz says.

"You weren't invited over, asshole," I say, even though I'm thinking about cooking for him. "And I'm not fucking around with your sister."

"What the fuck would you call it, asshole?" Harry bites out as he flexes his hands, then fists them. The bastard has a mean right hook. I don't answer because I am trying to decide how mad Allison will be when I kick her brother's ass. "Aren't you going to answer me?"

I look at him, a man I think of as a brother, a man I would go into battle with—have done before and would do again without thinking—and the anger I see in his eyes. I should have never touched her, but I couldn't stop myself. Not last night. Not this morning. Not for the rest of our days.

I know that I should back off. She's definitely too good for me, but now that I've had her, there will be no way for me to ever retreat. She's that sunshine I need in my world. I just can't go back into that role of friend. Not now. Not ever. So, I decide I have no choice but to tell him the truth. It's time I laid my soul bare to him, because I need him to understand what she means to me.

"I love her."

His eyes widen. "What the fuck?"

"Love, Harry. Like when I wake up, I can't think of anything else. All day long she's there, on my mind, in my soul. When I fall asleep, she's still there. All. Fucking. Day."

The silence that fills the kitchen almost deafens me. Fritz is unusually quiet, and I want to look at him, but refuse to look away from Harry. The silence ticks on for a few seconds before Harry responds.

"How long?" he demands, his facial expression giving nothing away.

I blink. "What?"

"How long has this been going on?"

"This morning."

He rolls his eyes. "No. How long have you felt this way?'

"Oh." It takes me a minute to gather the courage to admit it, but there's no going back now. "Since we moved to San Antonio."

He studies me. There's a look in his eyes I can't decipher.

"Like love?" he asks. "*Real* love?"

I nod, my patience wearing thin. I want them gone. I want to go back to my quiet morning of great sex with the woman I love.

"Ed," he says, and I can tell he's about to argue with me, like I'm not worthy of love or something. Panic forces me to lay my cards down on the table.

"I. Love. Her. Like put a ring on it, have a ton of babies, until we perish kind of love."

Again, silence descends on the kitchen as we continue to stare each other.

Fritz clears his throat. I look up and see Allison standing there, her face is pale, and her eyes are wet. Dammit, this wasn't the way I wanted to let her know how I feel. She should have been told first, and that had been my plan right before Harry found us.

"Fucking Harry," I mutter.

"Is that what you were going to say to me when Harry ruined everything?"

"Hey," her brother says, but I hear the laughter in his voice. I don't look at him. I only look at her, the whole reason I exist. The woman who is now crying in her kitchen.

I walk toward her, cup her face and wipe her tears away with my thumbs. "Don't cry, Sunshine."

"Tell me," she says, wrapping her delicate fingers around my wrists.

"I love you."

There is a second or two of silence, then her mouth curves and a fresh set of tears spill from her eyes. "Good, because I love you too."

I dip my head and kiss her. She slips her hands up over my shoulders, then behind my neck.

"Ack, that's gross," Harry says, which causes us both to start laughing.

I slip my arm over her shoulders. "No longer going to kick my ass?"

Harry shakes his head. "Can't. I'm afraid of Allison."

She laughs. "You should be. Loser."

"Yeah, yeah, love and crap. The important question is...when am I getting some French toast?" Fritz asks. "And, just so you know, EJ is expecting some. Savannah's text says she's dead and that her funeral is Wednesday."

"What's that about?" I ask.

"She had about two or three margaritas more than we

had. And at least three more shots. Besides, she has to work today."

"No wonder Austin was freaking out last night."

She nods. Fritz's phone pings again.

"Again, EJ wants confirmation of French toast or she's going to run by Whataburger for taquitos."

I roll my eyes. "Tell her I'm making more French toast. That way you all can eat, and Harry can tell us why he's such a grumpy ass after a night out at a woman's house."

"I didn't say we went to her house," Harry says as he grabs a mug.

"If you had been at your house, you would have changed," Allison says.

"Yeah, well, not everything is what you think it is."

"Dammit, Harry, now I want to know more about your date and that almost never happens."

"Except when you tried to set him up with EJ," I offer.

"Date From Hell," Harry mutters in the same tone that EJ uses when she speaks of the date.

"Still," Allison says.

"I'll tell you what, Allison," Harry says.

"What?" she asks just a little too sweetly. I know that tone and Harry should too, but he's a little full of himself today.

"I'll tell you about what happened last night if you can tell me how long you've been in love with Ed."

I glance over my shoulder. I know the answer to this,

but I can see the flush to her cheeks. Harry knows she doesn't want to admit to her teenage crush.

She opens her mouth to start a new round of arguments and I turn back around, the feeling of happiness filling my entire world. I listen to the siblings argue, a smile curving my lips as I start the batter for the toast. It might not have been my plan to spend the morning with my two best friends and the woman I love, but damn if it doesn't just feel right.

Chapter Thirteen

Allison

Hours after we finish breakfast, I wake up in bed. I'd been so sleepy after we made love again, I passed out. Looking at the shadows in my room, I'm pretty sure it's after five in the evening. I sit up and realize I'm still naked. I can't fight the grin that curves my lips, or the feeling of joy that fills me. I've turned into some kind of sex maniac, but I'm pretty sure Ed is okay with that.

Speaking of Ed, I look around and notice that his shirt is still on the floor where he tossed it when we returned to the bedroom. I lean over the side of the bed to grab it and fight back a groan. There are muscles that ache I'm not sure I've ever used before. After pulling on his shirt, I go in search of Ed.

I find him in the kitchen again. I have a feeling that is going to be something that will happen a lot. And that thought has my heart bursting. The man *does* look good in my kitchen.

He's working on frosting, from the looks of it. I lean up against the doorjamb and watch him. I don't think I could ever find him more attractive, but right now, with the sun streaming through the window, a smear of chocolate on his jeans...he's perfect. Just damned perfect.

"Are you going to keep staring at me?" he asks with a smile kicking up one side of his mouth.

"If I want to," I sass back.

He glances up at me, his eyes dancing. "Sorry, I woke up and wanted to let you rest a little bit, so I came in here."

"I'm not complaining. What kind of frosting are you making?" His eyebrows rise up and I roll my eyes. "I'm not good at baking, but I know the smell of frosting."

He finishes whipping the concoction, then sets it on the counter. "Buttercream with a little Grand Marnier in it."

I walk over to him; he watches my every move. His eyes warm as I get closer. The hum of need courses through my body. I don't think I'll ever be able to see that look on his face and not want to jump his bones. Still, I want these quiet moments along with all the insanity that seems to make me lose my mind.

"You look good in my shirt." His voice deepens over the words, his arousal easy to hear. It's down to the overwhelming insanity that seems to grip both of us on a regular basis.

"Thank you. May I?" I ask, nodding towards the bowl of frosting.

He nods, and I dip two fingers into the frosting. He's

watching me, his gaze locked on my fingers as I bring them up to my mouth. The scent of orange and sugar first hit my senses before I lick the frosting from my fingers. I hum, unable to fight the pure pleasure that winds its way through me. Sugar, orange, and another element. Something that is almost primal, that speaks to a part of me I don't truly understand. Ed. I realize now that every time I taste one of his creations, there is a part of him in it that I can taste. I know it's crazy, but I feel it in my soul.

Without asking permission, I move to get another bite of frosting.

"Nope," Ed says pulling the bowl away from me. Then, he leans down, picks me up, practically throwing me over his shoulder. He walks out of the kitchen and down the hallway to my bedroom.

"Ed, what are you up to?"

"If you think I am going to embarrass myself by watching you lick frosting off your fingers, you have another think coming."

"Embarrass yourself?"

"Yeah. I've got a hair trigger when it comes to you. If I come in my pants, I'll never forgive myself."

Before I can process that comment, he drops me on the bed just like earlier. It surprises a giggle out of me, that insanity is winding its way through me. It makes me crazy, but it also makes me so damned happy. For a second or two, he stares at me like before.

"What?"

He shakes his head.

"Ed, tell me."

"Your happiness makes you the most beautiful woman in the world."

I can feel my face flush. "Ed..."

I don't know what else to say to him. Not right now, not while he's staring at me as if I am the most precious thing in the world.

"You are." I open my mouth to say something funny, anything; because I'll cry happy tears otherwise. "Why would you think you aren't?"

I shrug. "I don't know. Men have never talked to me like that."

"Assholes. Well, that shit's over. Now you get the Ed treatment."

I smile. "What's that?"

"Well, you got a taste of it this morning but now we have this frosting." He wiggles his eyebrows at me as a sinful smile curves his lips. Did I say I was hot before? I wasn't. I don't think I've ever been *this* hot in my life.

"Yeah?" I smile. "And just what does that mean?"

He settles one knee on the mattress. "It means that I can find out just what frosting tastes like when I lick it off you."

Jesus. How have I not come just from talking to him? I have no idea.

"And," he says cocking his head to the side, "I think I have to ask for my shirt back."

"Is that a fact?"

He nods. "Give it up, Sunshine."

I don't hesitate to pull the shirt off me and throwing it off the side of the bed. I let my gaze travel down his body.

The tattoos scare a lot of stupid women away—thank God—but how has a piece of man meat like this been by himself for almost two years? He might be in his mid-thirties, but he's even sexier than when I first met him. Sculpted muscles, a few scars here and there from his time in the service, and those abs. I let my attention drift lower, Lordy. The outline of his cock is easy to see, and I reach for him, but he smacks my hand away.

"Nope. Frosting first."

I pout. "Why can't I use frosting?"

He closes his eyes and draws in a deep breath. "Good lord." He opens his eyes and looks down at me. "You might just kill me."

I bite my lower lip and fight another smile. Joy fills me as he sets the frosting on the bedside table. After dipping a finger into the bowl, he leans closer and kisses me. It shouldn't make me almost melt but it does. See, sexy...all Ed. Just the simple act has my heart turning over. He pulls back from the kiss before I'm ready for him to leave. Of course, he has other things on his mind. Mainly the frosting. He presses his frosting-covered finger over my nipple. As he smears it around, he raises his gaze to lock it with mine.

"I've always wanted to taste frosted Sunshine."

I can't look away from him as he bends his head and licks the hardened tip, encircling it with his tongue. His eyes drift closed as he sucks my nipple into his mouth completely. God. Liquid heat fills my pussy while he continues to lick and suck frosting from my nipple. My clit begs for attention, but he does nothing else than tease my nipple, before grabbing some more frosting for my other nipple. Every little lick and nip increase the need now pulsing through me.

He slides a frosting-covered digit down my stomach, before pressing the flat of his tongue against my flesh as he eats it up. As he inches closer to my mound, I can feel my clit throb in time with my heart.

"Now," he says, the gravelly voice causing my body heat to rise by about a bazillion degrees—and yes, I know that's insane, but right now, this is about me, so suck it. "That frosting is yummy, but not as yummy as pure, aroused Allison."

He settles between my legs and slips his hands beneath my rear end. He lifts me up, draws in a deep breath and his eyes slide closed again. "I wish I could bottle this up. I'd be a millionaire."

Before I can say anything about that, he lowers his mouth to my sex. His tongue traces my slit before it slips between the folds. He uses his nose to press against my clit, and I can't fight the moan that rises up out of my throat. It's loud, especially in my quiet house. He sighs against me, the puff of air adding another element to his efforts. The soft touch of his beard against my inner thighs and against my pussy is enough to make me come. Add to that the talented mouth and...good lord...I'm amazed I haven't lost it completely. I teeter on the edge, ready to fall, when he pulls away. I growl—actually growl —and he smiles down at me. I open my mouth to complain, but he flips me over on my stomach. The move is so fast, I can't seem to wrap my mind around it. It's kind of hard to think when all my brain cells have abandoned me in hopes of an orgasm.

I push up on my elbows, as he reaches over and grabs some more frosting. His fingers skim down my spine. His mouth follows. I need to come. The frustration now pounds through me and I want—no *need*—to come. I have no way to accomplish that. He has my hips anchored down with his hands now as he licks down my back. I collapse on the bed, my head in the pillows, but it doesn't help much with muffling the volume of my moans.

Then, I feel his teeth graze over one butt cheek before he moves again for frosting. Another smear and more licking. I might just die right here on my bed. I don't know how I can deal with the need currently beating through my blood, my body begging for relief. It's then that I realize I've been doing just that by repeating please over and over.

"Don't worry, baby, I'll take care of you," he says as he moves away for a second. I hear him undress before my brain computes what's happening. I open my eyes and look at him. Damn, the man is a piece of work. His cock bobs up against his stomach, hard and wet with a little precum. I want a taste, a little nip at his essence.

I reach out and press my thumb against the tip and bring it back to my mouth. Salty, sweet, Ed. God. I close my eyes and moan.

"Woman, I am barely holding it together," he says, which pulls a laugh from me. When the bed dips, I open my eyes as he crawls back up on it with me. The crinkle of foil tells me he grabbed a condom. I hate having it between us, since I'd enjoyed our time without one. Still, I know it's for the best, and the thought evaporates as he takes hold of my hips, pulls them off the mattress, and enters me to the hilt in one, hard thrust. We moan together as he holds us there, immobile for a few seconds. I can feel my clit pulsing, his cock throbbing, and Jesus, I just need to come. I struggle to my knees as he starts to move. His fingers dig into my flesh and he continues to thrust in and out of me. I'm close, ready to come, but it feels as if it is just out of reach.

As his rhythm increases, he slips his hand around to press against my clit. "Come with me, Allison. Come on, baby."

I can't deny his request. He thrusts into me and I scream as I tumble over into pleasure and my orgasm racks my body. Ecstasy sparks through every inch of my soul with my first release rolling over into another one. Ed groans and drives into me once more, riding my orgasm, and gives up to his needs. He holds himself still inside of me as he shudders.

Moments later, he collapses on the bed beside me. I still have my face buried in the pillows and he's facing up.

"I think I might need some rest after that one, Sunshine."

"I might be dead," I say, joking but only a little. Right now, I'm so drained I don't want to move for the rest of the day.

He chuckles, the warm sound making my heart dance. "I hope not, because I would not want to explain to your mother that I sexed you to death."

I laugh and move my head so I can see him. His eyes are closed, but there is no denying the smile on his lips. "I only ask one thing from you."

"What's that?"

"I get to use the frosting next time."

He opens his eyes and looks at me. "Anything you want, Sunshine. I love you."

"I love you, too," I say, my heart now filled to bursting. No matter how we figure this all out, we will figure it out together. He leans over and gives me a kiss, then slips out of bed. He removes the condom and tosses it in the trash before he rejoins me on the bed.

"Nap," he says, as he pulls the blanket up over us. He wraps his arm around me, pulling me close to him, letting me settle my head on his chest. "Then we go for a ride."

That sounds fantastic to me, so I do. As I drift off to sleep, I feel his lips against the top of my head.

Nothing could be better than Ed Cooper in my bed.

Epilogue

Three months later

I'm trying my best to keep my head on straight, but today is special. It's three months—minus one—to the day since I told Allison I loved her. And it's time. Because I can't wait any longer. This woman is my entire world and I want to make it official.

I'm in our backyard. Yeah, I moved in about a week after her staycation. Didn't wait to be asked. Just told her I would move in. She agreed, and while we have had a few bumps here and there, we definitely know we belong together.

Allison is on her way home. She knows I'm up to something, since I gave her a Saturday splurge fest complete with a day at the spa with her friends. Still, I have a feeling she has no idea what I am up to now. I have the backyard ready to go as the sun starts to descend over the Texas sky, but I have kept everything under wraps. Thanks to Savannah and EJ, I have the entire backyard decorated. Little fairy lights crisscross over the back porch, and I have candles on the table. I'm not that good with enchiladas, so I had Savannah make some up and they are ready to put in the oven.

EJ: *Hey, GJ, dropping your woman off. You are one lucky man.*

Yes, all of her friends call me Ginger Jesus or refer to me as GJ. I was annoyed and more than a little embarrassed at first. Now, though, I realize it is their way of accepting me.

Me: *Don't I know it.*

EJ: *:winky face:*

I hurry back into the house just as she is coming through the door. Sweet baby Jesus. The woman would be gorgeous to me no matter what she wears—although, I prefer her to be naked—but this dress takes my breath away. It's one of those kinds that tie behind her neck, leaving her back bare and dipping low enough to give me a great view of her cleavage. Her hair is softly curled into waves that make her look as if she has been sexed up. Her makeup is subtle, just a little here and there, except for the red lipstick. She looks like a pinup from the fifties.

"Ed?"

I shake my head and try to get my brain to work.

"What's wrong?" she asks.

"I just can't..." I draw in a deep breath, count backwards from ten, then do it three more times before I can continue. "You take my breath away."

Her expression clears as she walks towards me. "Thank you. You should see my lingerie."

I'm trying to hold it together and not lose it and rip that dress off her and have my way with her on the floor. She's not making it any easier. I can do this. I can hold my body in check until I get through everything I want to say.

She giggles. "Your expression is priceless."

I shake my head as I walk over to her. I cup her face, rubbing my thumb over her cheek. I'm careful not to mess up any of her makeup. That's for later. Right now, I want her to know just how much she means to me.

"Oh, no. What's wrong?"

I shake my head. "Nothing."

"There's something, Ed. Tell me."

A lump rises in my throat, and it takes every bit of my will to swallow it. "I love you."

Her expression softens. "I love you too, Ed."

"Be mine."

She blinks, confusion now clouding her eyes.

"I am yours."

I roll my eyes. "I'm doing this all wrong."

She smiles. "You never do anything wrong. Well, except when you put my purple sweater in the dryer."

I frown. "Just," I sigh.

"What? Spit it out."

I take her hand and pull her through the kitchen.

"Oh, are those Savannah's cheese enchiladas?"

"Yes."

But I don't stop. I pull her through the back door until we are on the tiny patio with all the candles. The sun is starting to set, and it was actually one of those rare cool summer days and the night is coming to life around us.

"Oh, Ed, this is so pretty," she says looking at the table. She looks at me. "Thank you."

"It's our three-month anniversary."

She nods. "I know."

For the first time in my adult life, my palms sweat. She is the one thing I need in my life and asking her this question scares the hell out me. Facing down the Taliban in a battle was never this frightening.

Allison watches me, waiting, anticipation stamped on her features.

"I saw your father today."

She nods and smiles. "That's nice."

I draw in another big breath and release it as I have her sit down.

"Three months ago, I told you that you were mine."

She nods.

"And I want to make it permanent."

"I'm not sure how much more permanent we could be. You're living with me."

She wasn't a stupid woman, but for some reason, she wasn't catching on. I slip my hand into my pocket and retrieve the ring EJ had helped me pick out two weeks ago.

Allison's gaze settles on the small velvet box. I open it and her eyes widen. I went all out, but not just boring diamonds, not for my Sunshine. I picked a princess cut diamond surrounded by sapphires, her birth month jewel.

"Be mine, Sunshine," I say. When she looks up at me, the shimmer of tears catches me off guard. I've upset her by asking her to be mine? "I'm sorry. Never mind. We'll live in sin for the rest of our lives."

Then the smile catches me off guard, and she rises from the chair. "Oh, Ed. I'm not upset by the proposal."

I pull her into my arms. "Then you need to stop crying."

She chuckles. "I'm just so stunned. I had no idea you were going to do this." She cups my face and looks me straight in the eye. "Yes, Ed. I'll be yours. I've been yours for the longest time, you just didn't know it."

Relief courses through me as I let go of a breath I didn't realize I had been holding. She leans closer as I dip my head. The kiss is brief, sweet, and very hot. I move back. I pull the ring out of the box and slip it on her finger. Perfect fit.

"It's so pretty," she says as she looks down at it. When her gaze raises to meet mine, I lower my head once more. This kiss is not sweet. It's carnal and wet, and Jesus, I go from a little aroused to almost full staff in a matter of seconds. It leaves me somewhat lightheaded. Probably because of the rush of blood to my cock.

I pull back. "Okay, dinner has to wait."

As I blow out the candles, she asks, "Why?"

I don't answer at first. Instead, I bend over and hoist her on my shoulder. The giggle causes me to stop for a second. My heart is ready to flop over onto the patio. The woman has held it in her tiny hands for so long, but now, we are together, the two of us, sharing this happy little house.

"You know, I can walk," she says, still laughing as I start back into the house.

"I know, but since this is how I took you to your room the first time, I figured it works."

She laughs as I carry her through our house, and into the rest of our lives.

Check out Luscious

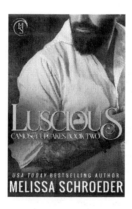

When by the book Harry Bradley gets thrown together with his sister's best friend EJ, opposites don't just attract, they explode.

UNEDITED

Chapter One
Harry

C hapter One
       Harry

The fine hairs on the back of my neck tingle and need clenches my gut. Without turning around, I know she has just stepped into our bakery. The woman I shouldn't be hung up on but dream about on a regular basis.

EJ. Elliana James. She hates her first name, opting to go by her initials. It's odd because her given name fits her. I've never met a woman who is so utterly feminine just like her name. From the long maxi dresses she wears, or the fact that she looks like the twenty-first century version of a 1950's bombshell, Elliana fits her to a "T". Still, I would never use the name again. I learned that lesson the hard way. The one time I did use it, she'd threatened to kill me. Not directly. Instead, she offered me a sweet, beautiful smile, and her eyes twinkled. Then she said, "It'd be a shame if Ed and Fritz have to run the shop without you. And your poor mama would miss you."

Her deep southern accent had dripped with honeysuckle sweetness, but there is no doubt in my mind she had just threatened my life.

Was that why my dick stood at attention every time she appeared? Probably. Mainly because I haven't been interested in a woman in the last six months—longer really. She's the only woman who drew my attention and made my blood beat with desire.

I roll my eyes. Jesus, now I sound like an idiot. Either way, the fact that a woman threatened me with bodily injury, and I sported a hard-on whenever I was around her made me one sick fuck.

I brace myself and turn around. She's smiling at me over the heads of some of the women in the shop. She's tall, so tall that when she wears heels, I wouldn't have to bend down to kiss her. For a guy who's over six three, that's a tantalizing idea.

I wait until she makes her way to the side of the counter through the bevy of women hanging out in line. One woman, a petite blond with permanent bitch face and the personality to match it, tosses EJ a nasty look. EJ seemingly ignores her except for the slight smile curving one side of her mouth. I know all her smiles and that's the one where she knows she's in charge.

Fuck, that's sexy.

"Harry," she says with that deep, sultry accent. I try not to fall down at her feet and beg her for a pet.

"EJ."

Her smile fades and I know I irritated her. It isn't that I *want* to irritate her. My flirting with EJ is part eight-year-old boy. I don't know what it is about her, but she makes me want to pull on her pigtails. Definitely immature and cliché, but I can't seem to control myself. Which, for me, is saying something.

"What do you need?"

"I was wondering if we could chat about working out an idea that would be beneficial to each of us."

"I don't know. Do you think we can?"

Her eyes narrow and I bite back my own smile. She might exude honey when she speaks, but there is nothing as sexy as EJ when she's mad at me.

Remember, I said I was a sick fuck. I am. Mainly when I'm thinking of EJ or in her presence or dreaming about her. Okay, anything to do with EJ leaves me frustrated and makes me act like a jerk.

She's my sister's best friend—well one of her two best friends—and she's come to me about business. EJ is one of the most formidable businesswomen I know. She's built Magnolia Books into one of the best stores in the south. That means something in this day and age, so I relent.

"Come on back to the office and we can chat."

She hesitates. I have to fight the need to demand she follow me. No one orders EJ to do anything, but I always want to.

With a sigh, she steps in my direction, so I know she's following. As we walk back to the small office we keep at the back of the bakery, I stamp down on my nerves. Or at least I try to. Doesn't always work. I step into the office, which is more like a glorified closet, and wait for her to walk through the door. The sweet scent of jasmine leaves my head spinning. After I close the door, I settle behind my desk as she sits in one of the two chairs in front of it.

EJ isn't a woman who asks for attention. She demands it with her way of dressing—the long maxi dress clings to her many curves—and her personality. The fact that she's a looker with her long red hair—I really want to know if she's a natural ginger—luminous greenish blue eyes, and those plump, pink lips doesn't help my infatuation. She's wearing just a sheen of pink lipstick and I want to smear it by kissing her. On top of that, she reminds me of a very tall Marilyn Monroe. I like the fact that she's curvy. Not that she cares, but, ya know—Just for reference.

"So, what can I do for you?"

She hesitates and that's not like EJ at all. I've always thought she would go into any situation full steam ahead and damn the consequences.

"I have a proposition for you."

I let one eyebrow rise up while I thank God that there's a desk between us. Otherwise, she'd know just how excited I am about her wording. I know better than to think she wants me in bed. We had one disastrous date that I know she calls *The Date From Hell*. She fidgets and again I note just how out of character that is for her.

"Go on," I say when the silence stretches out.

She sighs. "I have an idea about doing a few after hours events at the store."

EJ isn't just a beautiful face. She's a sharp business-woman who runs one of the most popular indie book-stores in San Antonio, if not the entire south. She's only been in business for three years, so I figure she'll dominate much of the US.

"Okay."

"Some of them will be themed, and I was thinking that I could work with Ed for some of them. Not all of them, but I know women and I know my clientele."

There was no doubt in that. She had built partner-ships with publishers and indie authors, focusing on romance and women's issues in her store. There was rarely a day that the store wasn't busy.

"Have you talked to Ed about this?"

She rolls her eyes. "You know what he's like. I can work out the food with him, but I need to make sure it's financially feasible for me to do. His head is always in powdered sugar clouds."

I chuckle. "Yeah, you're right about that."

Ed Cooper, my sister's fiancé, is a kick ass baker. He is the reason all three of them—Fritz being the third—started Camos and Cupcakes. Ed is good with the cupcakes and crappy with the business side of things. But that's okay, because that's my job.

"I was wondering if we could chat about this to see if we can work out something that's beneficial to both of our businesses."

"How so?"

"I know that Ed hired another part timer because he wants to branch out, yes?"

Of course she knew. Ed can't keep a secret from my sister Allison, and Allison always blabs it to her friends.

I nod.

She smiles and all of a sudden, I feel like I've won some award. Because a woman smiled at me. A woman who said I gave her the worst date of her life...and EJ dates *a lot*.

"I thought if we worked together, we could help Ed branch out. My clientele is mainly women and they tend to be in charge of things. In the home and in the office. They keep track of anniversaries, birthdays, and those kinds of things. I have a few more ideas that would be beneficial to both of us."

I see where she is going, and it is kind of brilliant. Low cost and hitting a market that might come in the shop to buy cupcakes or coffee but might not otherwise find out about our move into cakes.

"That's..."

"What?"

"It's a really fantastic idea, EJ."

For a second, something close to relief floods her expression but she soon banks it. "Great. So, I thought you could come over tonight."

"After you close?"

That's actually a good thing because I have last week's books to work on.

"Yeah, I thought I'd cook us dinner, and we could chat about it."

I blink. "You mean at your house?"

"Yeah. I work better with food in me and away from the store. I don't like eating too many of my meals there. It's a bad habit."

I nod because I understand that thought. Being self-employed wasn't as exciting when you had to handle all the business side of things.

"Not at a restaurant?"

She shakes her head. "I don't want people to be listening in. And I want us to be able to be honest. If we're out, there's always a chance we will be too polite."

I feel one side of my mouth kick up. "You've never been polite where I'm concerned."

She has the good grace to blush. "True, but this is business, and you know I don't mess around about that."

That's probably the one thing we agree on.

"Okay. Sounds like a plan."

Her face lightens and the smile she gives me is glorious. It's always hard for me to remember just how much she hates me when she smiles at me. Another wave of lightheadedness hits me. From a simple smile.

What would it be like to make her come?

Fuck me. I clear my throat, trying to push that idea out of my head.

"So, around seven?" she asks. I normally work out on Wednesday nights, but since she's offering me dinner, I'm happy to move things around to accommodate her.

"That'll give me enough time to drop off the deposit and close out receipts."

"That's what I was thinking," she says as she rises out of her chair. I do the same as my throat closes up. It's always like this when she leaves. I panic, for no reason whatsoever.

"Are you okay, Harry?"

Her Georgia accent dances over my name and I bite back a groan. Again.

I nod as I try to swallow. "Yeah, just a little tired."

"Wednesdays are the worst, aren't they? Everything slows down, people are kind of cranky because the weekend is so far away."

I nod.

"You remember where I live?"

I nod again.

"Well, back to work," she says. "See ya at seven."

Then she slips out the door. I drop into my seat and try to get my cock back under control because I know my friends, and they'll be back here in just a second or two. They do not disappoint.

"What was that about?" Ed asks.

"She's interested in doing some cross-promotion together."

Ed nods. "She mentioned it this weekend."

"You saw her this weekend? When?"

Okay, so I sound like a possessive jerk and worse, there is no reason for me to feel that way. He stares at me for a long time.

"She was over Sunday for breakfast."

"Oh."

"Is there something I should know about, Harry?" Ed asks as he sits in the chair EJ just vacated.

"No. What do you mean?"

One of his eyebrows rises up. The moment I met Ed in basic, I knew we would be friends. He'd told me I looked like an asshole. He's not far off. I've been lusting after a woman who wants nothing to do with me. Kind of makes me an asshole.

"You're kind of jumpy," Ed says studying me. I hate when he does that. He might be one of my best friends and my soon-to-be-brother-in-law, but he's also a busy body. Or he's become that way since he and my sister got involved.

"No, just that she caught me off guard, and that

wouldn't have happened if you had told me after you had breakfast with her."

"I didn't have breakfast with her. She came over to our house and had breakfast."

Our house. I'm mostly okay with it, especially now that they're engaged. But it's left me feeling a little...out of sorts. Not because they're involved. It's more that I envy them. My best friend and my sister. I know that it makes me more of a jerk. Shut up.

"Still, you didn't tell me about the idea."

"She didn't say much about it. Something about featuring our treats at her nighttime events. Authors like to have their books and cake when they come in. Easy to do and then we get all kinds of social media hits."

"Her idea?"

Ed nods. "She's a sharp one. I mean, she did dump your ass."

I grind my teeth. "She didn't dump me. We both hated every minute of that date."

Ed snorts. "Sure."

I push that aside. "Either way, we're going to do a little chatting about it tonight over dinner."

"Dinner? As in a date?" His eyebrows climb up.

"No." Not really.

"Don't mess this up."

"What?"

"Hey, what's going on?" Fritz O'Conner says as he steps into the office.

"Harry and EJ are having another date."

"We are not. We're going to talk about an idea she has for us to work together."

"You and EJ?" Fritz asks. "Bad idea."

I roll my shoulders, even though I know it's one of my tells. It's a sure sign that I'm irritated.

"No. Our store and Magnolia's."

Fritz frowns. "She has an idea for us to work together? What?"

I roll my eyes. "That's why we're getting together tonight. We'll go over the details. Apparently, she talked to Ginger Jesus and he forgot to mention it."

Ed frowns at me. He doesn't like it when we use Allison's nickname for him.

"What kind of ideas?" Fritz asks as he takes the last remaining seat. He's the face of the business. The pretty boy who can handle interviews and appearances without a problem. In fact, he gets off on it. Everyone loves him.

"She's starting to do some nighttime events and she wanted to have me do sweets for some of them. She also wants to coordinate social media or something like that."

Ed says it in a way that has both Fritz and I sharing a look. Ed was a first-rate soldier. The only other man I would want at my back would be Fritz. But, once he got into baking, he became obsessed. Granted, when they served together, it had saved their asses more than once. Now, though, he gets lost in ideas about new cupcakes.

"I was thinking we needed someone to manage our social media," Fritz says. He handles it now but none of them are very good at it.

"I'm not sure if we have that in the budget."

"I can get Avery to handle it. She's been doing it for a few businesses back in the Poteet area. At least, she can work with both of us to get it all squared away." Fritz's younger sister was kind of a social media know-it-all. She might just be perfect for teaching them.

"Great. Now, can both of you go fuck off because I have to get some work done since I'm meeting up with EJ tonight."

"Fine," Fritz says. "Just don't fuck it up."

"Yeah, what he said," Ed says. "I'll box up some cupcakes for you to take over. She likes those margarita cupcakes."

After they both leave, I should get right back to work. But I don't. Instead, I sit and think about EJ, our meeting and just why I can't get the woman out of my mind. I am not that kind of guy who obsesses over women. Business first, yes, but it's more of a respect. If a woman doesn't want anything to do with me, then walking away is a sign of respect. And I do have huge amounts of respect for EJ. So being a total asshole and having fantasies about her is just out of order.

I sigh and scrub a hand over my face. The sooner I get this all squared away, the sooner things get back in order.

About the Author

From an early age, USA Today Best-selling author Melissa loved to read. When she discovered the romance genre, she started to listen to the voices in her head. After years of following her AF Major husband around, she is happy to be settled in Northern Virginia surrounded by horses, wineries, and many, many Wegmans.

Keep up with Mel, her releases, and her appearances by subscribing to her NEWSLETTER or join in the fun with her Harmless Addicts!

Check out all her other books, family trees and other info at her website!
If you would want contact Mel, email her at:
melissa@melissaschroeder.net

instagram.com/melschro

amazon.com/author/melissa_schroeder

facebook.com/MelissaSchroederfanpage

twitter.com/melschroeder

pinterest.com/melissaschro

bookbub.com/authors/melissa-schroeder

Made in the USA
Lexington, KY
27 November 2019